D0467082

ALSO BY LESLIE MARGOLIS

We Are Party People

If I Were You

THE ANNABELLE UNLEASHED SERIES:

Boy Are Dogs

Girls Acting Catty

Everybody Bugs Out

One Tough Chick

Monkey Business

THE MAGGIE BROOKLYN MYSTERIES:

Girl's Best Friend

Vanishing Acts

Secrets at the Chocolate Mansion

ghosted

leslie margolis

ghosted

Farrar Straus Giroux
New York

MARGOLIS, LES

Farrar Straus Giroux Books for Young Readers
An imprint of Macmillan Publishing Group, LLC
175 Fifth Avenue, New York, NY 10010

Copyright © 2018 by Leslie Margolis
All rights reserved
Printed in the United States of America by
LSC Communications, Harrisonburg, Virginia
Designed by Elizabeth H. Clark
First edition, 2018
1 3 5 7 9 10 8 6 4 2

mackids.com

Library of Congress Cataloging-in-Publication Data

Names: Margolis, Leslie, author.
Title: Ghosted / Leslie Margolis.
Description: First edition. | New York : Farrar Straus Giroux, 2018. |
    Summary: After hitting her head, Ellie Charles, thirteen, encounters a
    mysterious girl who takes her to moments in her past that explain how
    she became a manipulative, unhappy person in a story reminiscent of
    Dickens' "A Christmas Carol."
Identifiers: LCCN 2017046445 | ISBN 9780374307561 (hardcover)
Subjects: | CYAC: Conduct of life—Fiction. | Middle schools—Fiction. |
    Schools—Fiction. | Family problems—Fiction.
Classification: LCC PZ7.M33568 Gho 2018 | DDC [Fic]—dc23
LC record available at https://lccn.loc.gov/2017046445

ISBN 978-0-374-30756-1 (hardcover) / ISBN 978-0-374-30763-9 (ebook)

Our books may be purchased in bulk for promotional, educational,
or business use. Please contact your local bookseller or the Macmillan
Corporate and Premium Sales Department at (800) 221-7945 ext. 5442
or by e-mail at MacmillanSpecialMarkets@macmillan.com.

For Lucy and Leo

ghosted

chapter one

News flash: It's not easy being perfect. It's actually a massively huge burden being the smartest, prettiest, best-dressed, and most popular kid at Lincoln Heights Middle School. But somehow I manage. And it's a good thing I do.

The kids at my school are like sheep. They need someone to follow. Otherwise they'd simply wander around, lost on some disgusting, smelly, old farm, or whatever it is sheep do all day long. Who knows? Who cares? Not me.

My point is this: The vast majority of my classmates crave someone to look up to, someone who is excellent at telling people what to do, how to think, and why their haircut is hideous. I am that lucky person: Ellie Charles, in charge of, well, pretty much everything that matters here at Lincoln Heights Middle School.

Need a visual? My hair is long and wavy and caramel with natural golden highlights. My eyes are greenish blue, kind of like an arctic tundra, except icier. I have dimples when I smile, which is most of the time, because, duh, why wouldn't I always smile when I've got so much going for me? My teeth are perfectly straight and white and I never even needed braces. I don't wear glasses, either.

Of course I get straight As, but they don't come easily. I work for them and I work hard, studying for a minimum of three straight hours every single night. If my teachers don't give me enough homework, I make up my own: memorizing all the state capitals, or inventing random math problems like 173 times 465 divided by two. The answer is 40,222.5. I did that right now, in my head.

I'm like a human calculator except way cuter, and with a much better wardrobe.

You think I'm lying?

Guess what?

I don't care what you think. I've got more important things to worry about.

It's 3:15, and the end-of-the-day bell just rang. The halls are crazy frantic. Kids are yelling and running and practically bouncing off the walls with energy. Tonight is the Winter Holiday Semiformal. This dance is the most important event of the school year, not including graduation, and it's fewer than four hours away.

As president of the student council, chairperson of the dance committee, and soon-to-be valedictorian, it's my responsibility to make sure everything is perfect. This has got to be the greatest school dance in the history of school dances—not simply at Lincoln Heights Middle School. I mean school dances everywhere, in the whole entire universe, so when you Google *best middle school dance* after tonight, you'll see pictures of my handiwork.

The pressure is on and everything starts now.

I throw open the double doors to the gym and waltz on in.

The entire committee is already there and waiting— fourteen kids, personally selected and trained by yours truly, except not one of them seems to notice my entrance.

Big problem.

I slip into the one empty seat in the circle of chairs, in between two of my besties—Sofia Green and Harper

Delany. Both of them are staring at their phones, zombie-like. They don't even glance in my direction.

I groan loudly. "Ugh, what is that horrible smell? Who farted?" I cup my nose with one hand, and wave my other hand in front of my face.

The random chatter stops. Now everyone's eyes are on me—like they should be.

"You all smell that, don't you?" I ask, surveying the room. Some people nod. Others look confused. Most of them squirm in their chairs, fearfully. Except wait a second . . . not everyone is paying attention. Jeremy Hinkey is still doodling on the cover of his notebook with a black Sharpie, completely ignoring me. I narrow my eyes and point at him. "It was you, wasn't it, Germ-y?"

He looks up, startled. Soon confusion gives way to terror. Much better. "W-w-w-what?" he asks, his voice trembling.

"That smell. You farted—and I'm not talking about some innocent little blip. This was a 'silent-but-deadly' and you look so guilty right now. You may as well save us the time and admit it."

He shakes his head furiously. "No, I didn't fart. I don't even smell anything."

"Well of course you're going to deny it," I say, pointing out the obvious. "Because farting in public is disgusting, right?"

"Yeah," says Jeremy. "But I—"

I cut him off before he can finish. "Thank you for finally speaking the truth, Germ-y. Don't you feel so much better now?"

Everyone else in the room cracks up, but I raise my hand to silence them. "Excessive flatulence is no laughing matter, people. It's a serious medical condition. Germ-y, as a concerned citizen and friend, I strongly urge you to call your doctor immediately."

"But I don't have a problem," Jeremy insists. "I didn't even fart. It wasn't me."

I shake my head. "I cannot deal with this now. You are totally distracting everyone and we have a lot to do, so just get out of here."

Jeremy's face is bright red. His eyes are glassy and he's blinking furiously, as if trying to hold back tears. "B-b-b-but you can't kick me off the committee. I'm helping with the decorations."

I sigh loudly and dramatically. "No, you *were* helping with the decorations. Now you are free to leave. And don't bother coming back tonight."

"Wait, what? You can't ban me from the dance," Jeremy replies, standing up.

"Not officially," I say. "But if I were you, I'd steer clear."

Jeremy opens his mouth to argue, but no words come out. He's speechless—finally. And he's actually crying.

Here's a secret: I love making people cry.

But I am careful to hide my joy, keeping my expression neutral, even slightly disapproving.

Kids stare in horror and disgust. Emmett and Chiara, who happen to be sitting next to him, actually inch their chairs away, as if being a loser is contagious. And who am I kidding? Of course it is.

When Jeremy finally realizes he's got zero chance of winning this argument, that things can only get worse for him, he picks up his grubby old backpack, slings it over his shoulder, and bolts out of the gym.

"Don't let the door hit you on your way out!" I call. Except it's too late. The door actually does hit Jeremy on his way out. Perfect.

I could take things further, make some sort of mean joke, but there's no point. I turn to the remaining kids. "Guys, I'm so sorry you had to see and smell that ugliness. I'm sure Jeremy is totally mortified. Poor guy. I'm going to call him later and check up on him, make sure he comes to the dance tonight. Everyone deserves a second chance. And I do hope he calls his doctor in the meantime."

"That's so nice of you," Sofia says. She reaches out and pats my knee.

Harper pats my other knee.

I nod.

Lily Brenner and Maddie Meyer, my two other best friends, nod along with me.

Actually, the entire room is nodding, possibly out of fear, but I have no problem with that.

"It's the least I can do," I tell everyone, with an exaggerated shrug. And it's true.

Because here's another secret: Jeremy is innocent. Pretty much everyone is. Yup, that's right, no one actually farted, at least as far as I can smell. But my plan totally worked.

Now that I have everyone's attention, I open up my notebook and begin. "Okay, we have three hours to turn this dingy little excuse for a gym into a magical winter wonderland. Everyone turn off your phones, and I mean power *off*. Switching them to silent mode isn't good enough because I'll still hear them vibrate, which could not be more annoying, okay? I'll wait."

Everyone pulls their phones from their back pockets

and purses and book bags and turns them off. Once they are done I say, "Now let's get to work. Adam Weatherby—what's going on with snacks?"

"Oh, that's me!" Adam stands, not realizing he's got his three-ring binder on his lap. It slips off and snaps open when it hits the ground. Pages scatter. He gasps as he looks at the mess, cheeks burning up in embarrassment.

Totally tragic.

I notice a math test among the mess of papers, a red C+ scrawled across the top. Reaching down, I pick it up with two fingers, crinkle my nose as if it's a rotten banana peel dipped in raw sewage, and hand it over. "Here you go, dude. Sorry you didn't do better."

Somehow Adam turns even redder.

I love it.

A few people giggle. Normally this would be an awesome thing to laugh about, but we don't have enough time. There's too much to do. So I give them my best dagger-eyed stare—silencing everyone.

"Come on, Adam, get it together," I say sharply.

"Sorry." Adam crouches down to sort out the mess he made, but he's taking much too long.

"We're not going to wait all day," I snap.

"Right. Sorry. I'm so sorry, Ellie. I don't know how that happened. I guess I just got nervous because—"

I cut him off. "Stop babbling. There's no time." Weakness can be so annoying. I don't even bother rolling my eyes because he is not worth the effort. "Forget it, Adam. Someone else. Tell me what's going on."

"No, wait. I've got it." Adam sits back in his chair and holds up a piece of paper, desperate to please. "Because of allergies, food sensitivities, and dietary preferences, Principal Gayle says we have to avoid meat and dairy and nuts and processed sugar and gluten. So that leaves us with raw veggies, sliced fruit, and unsalted popcorn."

"Which raw veggies?" I ask, raising my left eyebrow.

"Um, carrots, cucumbers, celery, and bell peppers?" he says nervously. Like he isn't even sure those are actual vegetables. "I bought bell peppers in three different colors—red, yellow, and orange."

Poor guy is so eager to please he sounds pathetic, desperate. This makes me so very happy.

"And what fruit?" I ask.

"Apples and oranges?" he asks, squirming in his seat.

"Are you asking me or telling me?" I bark.

"Telling you," he says with a nervous nod. "We're bringing apples and oranges."

"Aren't you forgetting something?" I ask.

Adam has no idea what I'm talking about. I can tell by the panicky stare he is giving me. After fumbling a bit more with his notebook and crossing and then uncrossing his legs, he says, "Um, pears? I can probably swing some pears, as well."

"That's not what I mean," I say, voice raised, completely out of patience.

"Oh." He pauses for a moment and then says, "Thank you, Ellie. You are doing an amazing job. Seriously. Totally bang-up."

"Bang-up?" I ask.

"Sorry. Not bang-up. That's so, like, ten years ago. I am just super excited to be here on this committee with you. It's been fantastic and I—"

"You forgot beverages!" I scream, interrupting because who has time for this nonsense? Not me.

"Beverages?" he asks.

"Yes, you, Adam Smeathersby, are supposed to be in charge of snacks and beverages. It says so right here in my notes. Do you need me to read you my notes, Adam?"

"Oh yeah. I mean no." He takes a deep breath and starts over again. "I mean yes, I'm in charge of beverages. Of course I know that. I'm taking this job very seriously. And I figured because of the no-sugar thing, and our limited budget, all that's left is water."

"Well, obviously. But what kind of water?" I ask.

"What kind?" he asks nervously.

"Do I have to do everything?" I ask. "Wait, don't even answer that because I know the answer is yes, I do. I mean, come on, Adam. Who doesn't know that water with lemon is an option? They only serve it in every restaurant in America. Have you ever been to a restaurant, Adam?"

Adam stares at me, silent and dumbfounded. For someone who was already quite pasty, I didn't think it would be possible for him to turn paler, but he actually does.

"Well, have you?" I shout.

He finally coughs and asks, "Oh, is that a real question? Yes I have. I have been to a restaurant. I've been to many restaurants. Did you want me to name them? I'm not sure I remember every single one but I could try. I didn't realize that I was supposed to—"

"Stop babbling!" I tell him, out of patience.

"Sorry," he whispers, confused, and now on the verge of tears.

I sigh deeply. "Water with lemon and cucumber slices," I say. "Nothing says Winter Holiday Semiformal like lemon cucumber water, okay?"

"Sure, okay. Whatever you say, Ellie. Thank you."

"Moving on to decorations," I say, consulting my list. "Who's on snow?"

Darcy Peterson raises one hand tentatively, and then puts it down again. She's biting her bottom lip and she tucks her dark hair behind her ears. Darcy is always tucking her hair behind her ears.

"You with the ripped shirt," I say, pointing at her.

"Oh," she says, flustered, looking down at herself, running her fingers along the slight tear in the bottom of her T-shirt. "I didn't even realize my shirt was ripped."

"That's hard to believe," I mutter under my breath.

Sofia and Harper both hear me and giggle.

Darcy's eyes go wide. She knows I'm making fun of her. Well, of course she does. She can tell by the laughter. Even though she couldn't have heard what I said. That means she can't say anything in her own defense. Cool trick, huh?

I feel that rush of power, of people being afraid of me.

Here's something I learned a long time ago: The more horrible I am, the more people fear me, and the more people fear me, the more they respect me. And here at Lincoln Heights Middle School, they don't simply respect me, they actually kind of worship me. It's an infectious, beautiful kind of power.

"What were you saying?" I ask sharply, getting back to business.

Darcy smiles, unsure. "I have a ton of cotton balls that I've been gluing together. I'm thinking we can put them around the edges of the gym and they'll look like snow cover."

"I like it," I say.

"And I've been making origami snowflakes with this beautiful silver-and-blue sparkly paper. And then I found a whole slew of Styrofoam balls that we can string from the ceiling. Like snowballs, in a few different sizes. I've already threaded them together with invisible wire," she says. "I hope that's okay."

"It's great," I say. "Good job."

Just then, Lily raises her hand. "We've also got white twinkle lights we're going to string up everywhere. It'll be fantastic."

I nod. "And what about the walls?" I ask, looking toward the cluster of theater geeks.

There are five of them, all dressed in black and various shades of gray, like a uniform. They are skinny, gawky kids with pimples and braces. Two of them are girls in leggings and baggy sweaters: Dezi Arnold and Reese Jeffries. The other three are boys in skinny jeans and flannels: Jack Gonzales, Ryan Slater, and Charlie Nguyen.

"Okay, Dezi. Talk to me. What have you got?"

Dezi clears her throat and stands, pulling Jack along with her—probably for moral support because she's too chicken to face me alone. Even though she is nervous, she also seems just about ready to burst with enthusiasm. "You wanted winter wonderland, yes?" she asks. "So we got a gigantic roll of craft paper and made mountains and a forest and, well, take a look."

Suddenly Ryan and Charlie get up and unroll a gigantic scroll. It's six feet tall and super wide—practically large enough to cover an entire wall of the gym. The whole scene is breathtaking. I can tell they worked hard on this, painting snow-covered mountains studded with green, spiky pine trees. Fluffy white clouds float overhead against a sparkling blue sky. There are a few snowman families scattered throughout, all of them with orange carrot noses, twigs for limbs, top hats, and bright scarves tied around their little snowmen necks in green, orange, yellow, purple, and blue. Red bobsleds dot the landscape, racing down hills with smiling children inside. The detail astounds me. This mural is so much better than I thought it would be. These kids have real talent.

Not that I'm going to tell them. I stand up and move closer so I can get a better look. Also, so I can see them tremble and sweat. They are scared of my reaction, even though any idiot can tell this work is brilliant.

There is no question. I love it. But obviously I keep this fact to myself. In fact, I don't even let on that I approve of the thing.

"This is just one wall," I say, frowning.

"Yes, we have three more," Jack tells me.

I nod, keeping my face completely impartial. "Okay, this one is fine. It can stay," I tell them.

Ryan and Charlie exhale loudly. The guys were so nervous they were both holding their breath.

It's inspiring, generating this kind of fear. It gives me fuel, like food or water. Sometimes I think I need it more than oxygen.

"Okay, so let's see the others," I say.

They carefully roll up the first scroll and then swap it out for the next one, and then the next. All three of them are similar and beautiful—each a distinct winter wonderland I wish I could step into, even more magical than I could've imagined. It's going to transform the entire gym. These theater geeks really did amazing work.

"How long did this take you?" I wonder.

"About a month of working on it after school," says Reese. "And late nights."

"Weekends, too," Charlie adds.

"Yesterday I pretty much flunked a major history test, I think, but it was totally worth it," Jack says.

The others laugh. I can't tell if he's joking or not and I don't really care.

"Okay, let's see the fourth one," I say gruffly, so they don't forget who is in charge.

"We saved the best for last," Reese says, grinning like mad. She holds one end, while Jack pulls on the other, unraveling the scroll. And I can immediately tell what they are talking about. This last scene is different from the others. It's much more detailed. Sure, it's got the same mountains and trees, blue sky and clouds, but it's also got deer, and a family of bears in the background, and rabbits leaping across a snowy, sunlit field. It actually looks like a gigantic professional painting someone would see in a museum.

"What's this?" I ask, pointing to the animals.

"Oh, we added some woodland creatures. I thought it would be fun," says Reese with a shrug.

"You thought it would be fun?" I ask, both eyebrows raised.

She gulps. "Yup."

"You're right. It looks nice." I move forward, take a closer look. That's when I notice a few red birds circling one of the pine trees. "I've just got one question: Why birds? Because birds don't belong in a winter scene—most of them fly south for the winter, like old people," I say.

"Not every bird," says Jack. "I did some research on this because I wasn't sure about it, either. But it turns out there's the red crossbill, and the northern goshawk, and snow geese, all of which are depicted here in their natural habitat, so—"

I yawn, loud and exaggerated, and wave one hand in front of his face. "Yeah, that's enough of that, bird boy. The woodland creatures are one thing. I mean, sure, I wish you'd checked with me, but I appreciate the surprise. Birds, though? Yes, some of them stick around. I know that because I'm not stupid. But that doesn't mean we have to include them in a mural. Because it's still a total disconnect. They simply don't fit into our theme."

"Sure they do," says Jack, standing up straighter. "As I said before, they are winter birds. It's a thing."

I don't know where he gets the confidence and I don't like it, so I laugh in his face. "I'm not interested in the facts, nature boy. My point is, no one thinks winter wonderland and birds. The two concepts don't even belong in the same sentence, let alone on the same wall. It's totally going to ruin the entire thing. We can't use it."

"But we have to," says Reese.

"I'll be the judge of that," I reply, squinting closely at the final scroll. "And that snowman in the background? The one between the bear and that deer? He looks a little chubby."

Jack lets out a big laugh.

I whip my head around and glare at him. "What's so funny?" I ask sharply.

"Oh, sorry. I thought you were joking. You know. About the snowman being chubby."

"I would never joke about something like that," I reply. "Obesity is a serious problem in this country. Don't you people read the newspaper?"

No one answers or argues with me. Well of course they don't. They're too scared.

Reese and Jack are still holding up the scroll in front of me. I take hold of the top edge so I can get a closer look.

"Careful, you'll wrinkle it," says Reese.

I look at her and smile.

She grins back, all friendly. Too friendly, considering

that we are not, in fact, friends. She hardly knows me. And she's lucky I let her be on this committee.

Come to think of it, why did I let her join?

Her bad attitude is almost as offensive as her bad skin. Pimples cover her forehead, nose, and cheeks. Why didn't I notice that earlier?

"You're just messing with us, right, Ellie? I mean, you wouldn't make us waste this whole thing . . . ," she says. "We've worked so hard."

"Maybe we can paint over the birds," Jack offers helpfully, pathetically.

"But why should we have to?" asks Reese, standing up a little straighter, her voice getting slightly louder. "We spent so much time making them and they look really good. Plus, they belong in this landscape. Jack did the research. I know that you are in charge, Ellie, but there are fourteen other people on this committee."

"Thirteen, now that Jeremy 'Fartburger' had to go," I remind her.

Reese sighs and runs her fingers through her hair. "Fine. Thirteen. My point is, if most of us think it looks good, then we should keep it. Shouldn't we take a vote or something? I mean, why do you get to decide everything?"

Huh. People rarely stand up for themselves around

me, and to be challenged by Reese—a total nerd? It's so unexpected and kind of refreshing.

Kind of.

I don't say anything in response. Not at first. Instead, I put my other hand on the scroll.

Reese's smile starts to waver and she glances from my face to my hands.

Everyone is watching us, waiting for my next move.

The paper feels so flimsy. I'm suddenly overcome by an urge to destroy it.

Ripping it in half would be cruel, a truly terrible act. But then again, maybe these theater geeks deserve it. After all, they didn't ask me if they could include woodland creatures in the scene. And birds? How dumb. We're in eighth grade, not preschool. I could say as much, but actions speak louder than words . . .

As I contemplate what to do, I feel a gentle tug at the paper. Reese is trying to take it away from me, but subtly, as if I'm not even going to notice.

As if . . .

I pull in the opposite direction, softly at first. But then she tightens her grip, so I yank on it hard and it tears, making an angry ripping noise that reverberates throughout the gym.

Someone gasps.

Reese cries, "No!"

And it's too much for me, her being so precious about her work, about this slight tear at the top of the scroll. It's easily repairable, and even if we left it—no one would notice. I mean, who does she think she is? Michelangelo? Frida Kahlo? Van Gogh? This is nothing, certainly not enough to teach her a lesson. She wants to complain? I'll give her something to complain about.

I pull at it again, harder this time, so that the paper tears all the way. Now Reese is left holding one half of the scene, and I have the other. It's terrible. Truly awful, and exactly what I needed to do.

I look to Reese, challenging her. She is stunned and speechless. Her pale-blue eyes are wide and filling up with tears.

"It's okay," I hear Jack whisper. He puts a hand on her shoulder. "We can still tape it. No one will notice."

"You think?" I ask, as I take my half and tear it again, and again, and again, until it's merely a bunch of tiny pieces. Next, I throw it up over my head like confetti.

"Oops!" I say. "Well, at least we have more snow."

Sofia laughs, but it sounds forced. I shoot her an evil look—make a mental note to deal with her later.

Meanwhile, everyone else is silent, too stunned to make a sound.

Except for Reese, who is suddenly red-faced and fuming. "How could you?" she sputters, fists clenched at her sides.

Before I can answer her someone's phone starts to ring.

Unacceptable!

"Who left their cell phone on during my meeting?" I yell, spinning around.

No one says anything. I look toward the noise and realize the ring tone sounds familiar. Oh wow, it's coming from my purse. "Hah, that's me," I say. "Get to work, everyone. String those lights. Hang the murals. Put out the snow. Find something cool for the fourth wall. And someone grab the disco ball from the supply closet. I'll be back soon."

I grab my bag and step outside so I can answer my phone. The number on the screen is one I know, and it makes me happy.

"Hey, Daddy. What's up?" I ask once I'm in the hallway.

"Ellie, sweetie. How are you?"

I sigh and reply, "Fine. Tired. Running this dance has been exhausting. You wouldn't believe the incompetence I have to deal with."

My father chuckles and says, "That's the Ellie I know and love. I'm sure you will pull it off beautifully."

"Well, I have no choice now, do I? Who else is smart enough to be in charge of this whole thing?"

"No one, babe," my father assures me.

"It's just so stressful, and everyone is super annoying. I can't wait until this whole thing is over with and I'm in Hawaii," I tell him.

"You won't have to wait for long. I'm sending a car to pick you up at your mom's house at five a.m. tomorrow."

"A limo?" I ask.

My dad chuckles instead of answering.

I frown, not that he can see me. "I'm not joking," I tell him.

"Oh, Ellie. You're too much."

"I think I'm just enough," I reply. "It's bad enough that you are making me fly coach."

"Thirteen-year-olds don't need to fly first class, Ellie. If your life is too easy now, you'll have nothing to look forward to. No reason to work hard. And speaking of . . . how is school? Still at the top of your class?" he asks.

"Of course," I tell him.

"Well, good," my dad replies. "I can't wait for you to get to Maui. You are going to love it."

"You got me my own private suite, right?" I ask. "And it's overlooking the ocean?"

My dad laughs again. "Of course, sweetheart. This is a special occasion."

"You mean us finally spending Christmas together after so long?"

"Sure, that, and I also have another big surprise for you."

"Wait, what?" I ask. "What is it? You know I hate surprises."

"You're gonna love this one," my dad says. "You did clear this trip with your mother, correct?"

Ugh. I can't believe my dad is asking me this now, when there's so much going on. My parents split up years ago, and I almost always spend Christmas with my mom. Usually my dad is too busy with work stuff. He actually never takes vacations. Except this year is different. This year my dad invited me to Maui and there's no way I'm not going. The only catch is, he insisted that I be the one to break the news to my mom. They don't speak anymore. And I fully intended to tell her . . . eventually.

"Ellie?" my dad asks. "You still there?"

I glance back toward the gym, take a deep breath, and then lie. "Of course I told her."

"How'd she take the news?" he asks.

"Do you actually care?" I reply.

"Ellie, that's not fair," my dad says. "Your mother and I have our issues, but she's still your mom, and she deserves to be treated with—"

I sigh, cutting him off. "She's fine, and I've got to go."

"Okay. Can't wait to see you tomorrow."

"Yup, me too. Bye," I say, and hang up.

I peek into the gym. Everyone is bustling around, working together, getting stuff done. One of the murals is already up on the wall. Darcy and Jack and Adam are stringing snowballs from the basketball hoops. Maddie and Harper are putting up the snowflakes. Everyone has done an amazing amount of work in the time I've been gone. I'm impressed. I think about joining them, pitching in to help make everything go faster . . .

And then I realize that I still have to do my nails.

I just got this new polish called Winter's Chill, the shade of which will match my dress perfectly. It only takes a few minutes to do my fingers, but I need to wait a lot longer to make sure they are dry. So I head to the football field and power walk around the track a few times. It's chilly but I can take it.

As I exercise, I work on composing a note to my mom

in my head. I think brief and to the point is key. Something like, *Hi, Mom. Flying to Maui to see Dad. Merry Christmas. See you next week!*

Actually, I don't even need to put that in a note. I'll simply sneak out of the house before dawn and then text her from the airport. My mom will understand. I hardly ever get to see my dad. He travels a lot for work and his schedule is too unpredictable. It's been almost a year since we've spent time together, and he only invited me to Maui two weeks ago. How could I say no? I can't. This is a wonderful opportunity for me. I've never been to Hawaii, and my mom would never take me to a fancy resort, even if she could afford to. It's simply not her style. And sure, with me gone, she'll have to spend Christmas alone, but what's the big deal? It's only one stupid holiday.

I blow on my nails and test the polish, gently brushing my thumb along my pinky—all dry.

By the time I get back to the gym, the entire room has been transformed.

The twinkle lights run from each corner of the room and meet at the middle. The mounds of cotton balls are bunched together in a way that looks surprisingly like snow. The three murals I approved of are up and looking magnificent. On the fourth wall, they've hung the half of the scroll that Reese was able to save, except they painted over those stupid birds. Much better. They even scrounged together enough of Darcy's snow to cover the remaining part of the wall, so it looks kind of like a three-dimensional sledding hill.

"We're running out of time, people," I announce, checking my watch.

"We're almost done," Jack tells me, wiping some sweat off his forehead.

Behind him, Maddie and Lily are lugging the gigantic disco ball to the center of the room, where the big ladder is already set up.

Dezi follows them with a spool of invisible wire.

Jack starts climbing the ladder.

"What are you doing?" I ask.

He looks at me with panic in his eyes.

"Um, I thought I was doing what you wanted me to do," he says.

"No way, you've already screwed up the scenery. This disco ball is the centerpiece of the whole entire room. It ties everything together and *I'm* going to hang it up," I say, pushing him out of the way.

I cannot believe he is trying to do this last thing, steal the spotlight from me. It's completely unacceptable.

I grab the spool of wire with one hand, and carefully tuck the disco ball under my arm. It's not that heavy, but it's big and hard to manage. I awkwardly reach for the ladder with my free hand and start to climb. As I take my first step, I realize it's actually kind of rickety. "Someone hold this!" I shout.

Sofia and Reese run over and station themselves under me, each holding on to one side of the ladder.

"That's better," I say. "Now, don't let go."

I climb another step and then another. The higher I go, the more nervous I am. I've never been excited about heights, but I'm not going to let anyone know. Fear is a sign of weakness, and I am anything but weak.

I can handle this—it's only a disco ball. And once it's hung, the room will be perfect.

Taking a deep breath, I climb another rung.

"Be careful," Maddie calls up to me. I know she means well, but she sounds like a total nag. Could she actually know I'm afraid? Annoying.

"I'm fine," I bark down to her. "This is not a big deal."

I am feeling the opposite but hope no one can tell.

When I finally reach the top of the ladder I loop the wire around the middle of the beam and then tie on the disco ball.

There. Done. The ball is composed of hundreds of little square mirrors and as it spins, I see my image in miniature reflected back to me a hundred times. It's gorgeous. I'm gorgeous. But wait a second . . . Something is off.

"Is this thing centered?" I call down to the crowd below.

No one answers. I look at the ground, which seems so far away, and why isn't anyone paying any attention to me? "Hey, dummies! I asked you a question!" I shout.

A few people glance up at me: Maddie, Jack, Lily.

"Is it centered?" I call again, hardly believing how far away everyone looks from here. I hope no one notices the tremble in my voice. Who knew the gym ceiling was this high?

Jack shades his eyes with one hand and squints at me. "I can't really tell from where I'm standing," he says.

Ridiculous. I can't believe I have to do everything around here. I lean back a couple of inches, trying to get a better look because these marshmallows-for-brains kids can't tell me anything. And just as I suspected, it's slightly off.

I nudge the ball to the left barely an inch. The ball sways a bit and then steadies itself and now it seems perfect.

I'm about to make my way down the ladder when I notice something odd. The face in all those mirrors? It's not mine anymore. Instead I've been replaced by some other girl. She's got dark hair, bright blue eyes, and pale, freckly skin.

She's eerily familiar, and yet, I can't place her.

Of course, the more I stare the more I start to get this strange, unsettling sensation that I've seen her somewhere before. That in fact I know her well . . .

Then very suddenly, I startle and step back.

And that's when I remember I'm standing on a ladder.

I mean, I *was* standing on a ladder.

Everything that happens next seems to happen in slow motion.

It's the scariest sensation—kind of like being on a roller coaster that's flown off its track. You know things are going to be bad . . . it's simply a question of when, and to what degree.

For a few moments I seem to float in the air, breathless. And then I'm plunging down, down, down . . . speeding toward the gym floor.

I close my eyes.

I brace myself.

I crash-land.

Pain shoots through my entire body. As my head hits the floor I actually feel my brain rattle. I am . . . terrified, but more than that . . . furious.

And somehow this eclipses my pain, and actually energizes me.

I cannot believe they let me fall. My committee is full of morons. I can't decide who I'm going to scream at first, but I know it's going to be ugly. I ball up my fists and open up my eyes and spring to my feet.

"What is wrong with you people?" I shout. "Who let me fall? You guys are idiots and I hate you all!"

I scream and rant and pace back and forth, but, oddly, everyone ignores me. It's like they don't even hear me. Like they can't even see me.

That's when I realize that every single one of them is huddled around the spot where I fell.

"What is going on?" I shout, marching back over. I stop short a few feet away. Suddenly I feel cold, an intense chill that radiates out through my limbs from my chest. It's because I see something in front of me.

Something crazy that makes no sense whatsoever.

It's a body.

Inching closer, I realize it's not simply any old body.

It's *my* body. Even though I'm standing up, somehow I'm also still lying there on the gym floor, just a little to the left of the half court line. My eyes are closed. I'm on my back. Legs and arms askew, body motionless. Nails still perfect.

Except, I'm also standing here outside of my dance committee's huddle.

I am standing up and I feel fine, which makes no sense at all because I happen to be staring at my own body on the ground.

It's like I'm two people now.

But how can that be?

Unless . . .

Wait a second . . .

Have I died?

chapter two

"You're not dead, stupid."

This from the girl who is suddenly standing next to me. She has appeared out of nowhere and she's got radiant black hair, bright blue eyes, and freckles across the bridge of her pert little nose. She's dressed completely in black: black tank top, black pants, black shiny high-heeled boots. She's even wearing a skinny black scarf around her pale, white neck. Unlike the theater geeks, on her these clothes look amazing. Maybe it's because she's older and gorgeous. Or maybe it's the slash of red lipstick, her long, thick eyelashes, and the mischievous glint in her eyes.

She also looks familiar somehow. Was hers the face I

saw in the disco ball? I am so confused. My brain actually aches. And this entire scenario is completely nuts.

"Then what's going on?" I ask, my voice warbling and shaky with nerves. "Am I a ghost?"

"Not exactly," she tells me. A know-it-all, this one. "You're simply . . . invisible."

She says this last bit in a spooky voice, except not true spooky—more like an exaggerated spooky voice, the kind you'd use on a little kid. She's making fun of me, but only subtly. This girl is tough and sharp as nails and rude with a capital R. She reminds me of someone: myself. And I don't like it. I put my hands on my hips and give her my best evil eye.

"But how? And why? And who are you, anyway? How come you can see me? And how come they can't see you?" I ask.

Because I've just noticed that we are having a very loud conversation while everyone else in the gym is acting as if we do not even exist. My entire committee is still standing over my body. The one that remains on the floor, I mean.

"And why are there two of me?" I ask, more softly this time.

She shrugs, as if bored by my torrent of questions.

Then she gestures toward my Winter Holiday Semiformal Dance committee. All those kids now milling around, whispering to one another, worried expressions on their faces. "As far as they're concerned, we aren't even here," she informs me.

"How is that possible?" I ask, letting my guard down for a moment because I am genuinely curious.

"It merely is," she replies.

This makes no sense, and now I'm annoyed again. "That's not really an answer," I tell her pointedly.

She smirks. She couldn't care less if she tried.

Normally, I would almost respect that kind of behavior, but now? There is no way. There's too much at stake.

I gesture toward my body on the floor and ask, "Is my soul still in there?"

The girl in black shoots me a sharp look and raises her finger to her lips. Then she nods toward the committee. "Hush up and listen!" she says.

So I do. Watching this scene unfold is kind of like seeing a movie of my life.

As far as the dance committee knows, the girl in black doesn't exist. And the only Ellie in the room is the one they are standing over.

I turn my attention to them, wondering how this is going to play out. Why aren't they doing anything?

Is it because my living, breathing, invisible-to-them body is about to fuse back to my dead-looking body so I can stand up and do some yelling? I hope so. The list of people I want to scream at keeps growing. This entire committee is looking so dumbfounded, and it is no coincidence that the word *dumbfounded* starts with *dumb*. I am so annoyed. "You guys are complete morons. Someone do something!" I scream, waving my arms frantically.

Not one of them even flinches. They are all so quiet. The only sound I hear is this girl in black, who stands off to the side, quietly giggling.

This is so frustrating. "Come on, people," I try, softer this time.

And then, finally, Maddie snaps to attention. "Someone call 911," she says.

"But she told us not to use our phones," Lily reminds everyone.

"That was before, and this is an emergency," Jack reasons. He's already got his phone in his hands and he's punching in numbers.

I'm glad someone has enough sense to know what to do in this situation.

"Thank you," I tell Jack. I'm standing right next to him, but he doesn't answer me or even look my way.

I tap him on the shoulder, but my hand goes right through his body. Creepy! Next, I try grabbing him by the shoulders, but the same thing happens. I'm grasping thin air. I'm like a hologram. Or maybe he's the hologram.

I put my hands in front of my face and wiggle my fingers. They look normal, solid, and lovely, of course. But then, when I try to poke Jack in the stomach, I can't. Instead I stumble forward, lose my footing, and fall into him. Except—surprise—I don't exactly bump into him. I move right through him and fall to the ground.

"What is going on?" I ask, scrambling to my feet.

I look to the girl in black. She rolls her eyes and says, "I told you so, dummy."

"What did you tell me and who are you calling a dummy?" I ask.

"If they can't see or hear you, then obviously they can't feel you, either," says the girl in black. "I thought it was obvious, but I guess I have to spell out everything for you."

I want to respond but I also don't want to miss what's happening, so I turn around in a huff.

Meanwhile, Reese is hunched over my body asking, "Do you think she's dead?"

"I'm sure she'll be fine," Darcy says, kneeling on the ground so she can get a better look. "She has to be fine." I hear true distress in her voice, which is somehow comforting.

"She came down so hard," says Adam, shuddering. "The whole gym seemed to vibrate."

"Wait, is he calling me fat?" I ask. "I'll totally get him for that later."

The girl in black glares at me yet again. "What part of 'hush up and listen' don't you understand?" she asks.

"Why do I have to be quiet when no one can hear me?" I ask her.

"I can hear you," the girl in black replies, and her voice could not be any snootier. "And I find you incredibly irritating."

Wow, this girl is brutally honest.

I don't love it, but I do respect it.

And it's probably a good idea to listen to her, at least for now. She does seem to know what's going on. I turn back to the scene.

"Is she breathing?" Harper asks.

Darcy lowers her ear to my chest and her eyes widen with panic. "I can't tell . . ."

Jack walks away from the crowd as he talks into his phone. "Yes, someone fell off a ladder in the Lincoln

Heights Middle School gym. She's unconscious. Please send help. And fast!" Jack pauses for a minute then responds, "Okay, I'll wait on the phone."

Good old Jack.

"Do we cancel the dance?" Maddie asks.

Lily shakes her head. "No way. She'll kill us if we cancel the dance."

"She'll kill us if we have the dance without her," Dezi points out.

"That's true," Lily chimes in.

"But, guys . . . ," says Reese. "What if she's already dead?"

My shoulders tremble because I suddenly have the chills.

No one has answered Reese. Everyone on my committee is staring at one another, wide-eyed with fear and confusion. Except for Maddie, who is checking her Instagram account, and Lily, who is sneaking M&M's from her pocket and eating them, right over my possibly dead, and definitely unconscious, body.

"How can you eat chocolate at a time like this?" I scream in her face, but the words don't even register.

"Um, have you already forgotten that they can't hear you?" asks the girl in black.

"No, I'm not stupid," I reply.

"Could've fooled me," she mumbles under her breath.

I don't argue because I need the girl in black on my side. She's the only one who understands what's going on. And things keep getting creepier by the minute.

Everyone is too silent.

Darcy hasn't confirmed that I am breathing. No one has.

I hear sirens in the distance.

This is too intense. I can't watch. I head away from my body, toward the girl in black. Except she isn't even looking at me anymore—she's staring down at her phone, texting.

"Um, excuse me," I say.

She looks up. "Yeah?"

"Are you my guardian angel?" I ask hopefully.

"Hah!" she replies, staring back down at her phone.

"Okay, from your mocking tone, I guess I'll take that as a no," I say, pausing and trying to process everything. I should've known. Sure, this girl is pretty and well dressed, but she is also way intimidating and rude. Any guardian angel of mine would at least pretend to like me. Isn't that the whole point of having a guardian angel?

I continue to puzzle this over and then suddenly it comes to me. I snap my fingers. "I know—you must be the Grim Reaper. That's why you're dressed in all black, right?"

She shakes her head, bored. "Look, if you really don't know who I am yet, and you've got to put a label on me, you can call me the Girl in Black."

Now I'm excited. "Wow, can you read my mind? Because that's exactly how I've been referring to you inside my head, which is so crazy. Do you have other powers, too? Because I—"

Before I can finish my thought, the Girl in Black holds up her hand and cuts me off.

"Hey, I've got a brilliant idea: Stop asking questions. Actually, stop talking completely. Keep your mouth shut and follow me."

She strides past my committee, past my lifeless-looking body, to the double doors of the gym, which she throws open. Then she turns around and motions for me to follow. "You coming?" she asks.

I glance at myself on the floor one last time. This is so creepy, so crazy. I am momentarily paralyzed, with no idea of what I should do.

The sirens are getting louder. Pretty soon the ambulance will show up, and I don't want to see what happens next.

I turn back to the Girl in Black. "Where are you going?" I ask.

"You'll see," she replies.

I'm scared to go with her, but I'm terrified to stay. So I follow.

chapter three

I'm close at her heels, but I don't bother asking any more questions of the mysterious Girl in Black because I know she won't answer me. Not now, anyway. She's made that clear. I'll simply try again later, once we're outside.

That's my plan, anyway.

Except when I walk through the double doors of the gym, I'm not outside and I don't even seem to be on campus. I am somewhere else—nowhere I've ever been before, I don't think, although it's hard to tell. Everything in front of me is so foggy, I have no idea where I am.

It's also warm.

Actually, it feels sort of toasty.

And the smell is a little too familiar. I inhale deeply, trying to figure it out. I'm not sure at first, but then it hits me. The air smells like freshly baked sourdough bread.

I know because my mom and I used to bake sourdough bread when I was little. Like on a weekly basis. For ages—since before I can remember. It's her thing. And it became my thing, too. Our thing. For a while, anyway.

As I'm remembering this, the wall, or whatever it is in front of me, opens up and now I can see through it. Sort of like a window. I'm looking at a kitchen with yellow plaid wallpaper.

The place is familiar. Something inside of me stirs. I sense that I have been here before, but a long time ago. And then it dawns on me—this is the wallpaper we used to have in our kitchen when I was a baby. My memory isn't that great, but I have seen a bunch of old pictures from those days.

Someone walks into the room. It's my mom. A younger version of my mom, that is. She's in jeans and an old ripped, blue T-shirt. Her hair is pulled into a messy bun on top of her head and she's wearing tortoiseshell glasses. She's carrying something on her hip. Someone, I mean. A baby with fuzzy blond hair and big greenish-blue eyes and chubby rosy cheeks. It's me.

My mom puts me in a high chair and kisses me on the forehead.

Then she bustles around the kitchen happily, unloading the dishwasher and wiping the counters clean and pulling some things out of the pantry: flour and an old mason jar. She puts them both on the counter and faces me, beaming.

"Guess what, Ellie? Today, we are going to start a new tradition. Are you ready? We're going to make sourdough bread. From scratch."

My mom is talking to baby me like I understand. I am watching, wide-eyed. I'm not even old enough to speak. Not really. Although I am banging a spoon against the table chanting, "Ba, ba, ba . . ." Which must be "bread."

"Can you say 'sourdough starter'?" my mom asks sweetly.

Baby me smiles up at her and says, "Ba!"

"Close enough!" my mom says, clapping. "Here is how you make sourdough starter: You mix flour and water. Then you wait. Tomorrow it'll start to grow and bubble. After twenty-four hours we throw away half and add more flour."

She looks at me to make sure I'm paying attention. I am rapt, but who knows what I actually comprehend. I guess it doesn't matter. She goes on explaining. "Then we wait some more. Then we split the starter, toss half, and feed the remaining part every twelve hours. It'll foam and bubble and start to smell tangy. And as it grows, it'll start to double in size every four to six hours. That's when you know it's done. We use half. We save half. We feed it once a week. And we will keep this starter forever. It's that simple. Every single loaf of bread we bake from now on will come from this starter. It'll take a week to grow and mature. And this is the beginning of us. Our family in this house. You can take this starter with you when you grow up and have your own house. It's hard to imagine, right? But that's what we're going to do. This is our beginning."

My mom puts the starter in the mason jar. It's got a blue top. Then she puts it in the fridge—in the door below the butter compartment. I know that container and I know that spot—it still lives there to this day. If I'm about one in this scene, and I'm thirteen now, that means this starter has been growing for twelve years.

Is this a memory or a dream? I wish I knew. It seems so real.

And just as I have that thought, the images disappear right before my eyes. The window closes up, and I'm in a strange tunnel.

I breathe in again. The scent is delicious and yet, alarming. Because what is this place? Why would it smell like the bread from my childhood? And how come everything in front of me is cream colored?

Also, everything around me feels kind of thick and slightly moist, which makes no sense. Unless . . .

Wait a minute.

It seems that I am not simply *smelling* sourdough bread, I am actually, somehow, in the middle of a freshly baked loaf. But how can I be motionless on the floor of the gymnasium, while at the same time, walking around and talking in the middle of what is apparently a loaf of bread? It makes no sense.

"Hello?" I shout.

No one answers. The Girl In Black is nowhere to be found. It seems that I am all alone. I keep walking through the loaf of bread because I don't know what else to do.

Have I shrunk to the size of an ant?

Or is this bread loaf gigantic?

This is the craziest dream I've ever had.

At least I hope I'm dreaming.

Soon an opening appears before me. It seems to be some sort of passageway and it's glowing.

Not knowing what else to do, I follow the path. And

then suddenly I see a glint of light. Many glints of light, that is. I move faster, closer, until I can make out their forms completely.

I'm now standing at the end of the tunnel in front of something sparkly and familiar: a pink and purple and silver beaded curtain. But it's not simply any old curtain. It's the one I had in my room a long, long time ago. When I was little. Before, well, before my whole world blew up.

It's been years since I've seen it. I scrapped the thing back when I turned ten, deeming it cheap and babyish.

Except here it is now: my beloved beaded curtain. I can tell it's the original one because there is a small gap near the end. The week I got the curtain, soon after I turned seven, I cut off several strands. I wasn't trying to destroy it—I loved that thing. It's more like the opposite—I wanted to have it with me always, not simply at home in my doorframe. I felt the need to wear it around my neck, all the time, as a necklace. For some reason, I didn't think anyone would notice the missing strands, but of course it was obvious. The curtain never looked the same, never looked as good. But I loved that thing despite its flaws. Even after I tore it down, I still missed it.

Not that I ever admitted that to anyone. Sentimentality is for the weak. That's a lesson I learned early on.

Anyway, the curtain: I honestly have not thought about the thing in years.

Curiosity forces my hand. I reach out and pull back the curtain. The strands move easily, making a familiar series of clicking sounds—beads knocking into one another. The sound is soothing. And this is interesting. Apparently, even though I cannot touch another human being, I can move objects, or at least this object—the beaded curtain.

How do double doors in the gymnasium lead to a sourdough bread tunnel that leads to the beaded curtain from my old room? I don't know, but feel the need to investigate. So I take a deep breath and walk through the curtain.

Sure enough, I find my childhood bedroom. Same pink shag carpet with a blue nail polish stain in the corner. Same rainbow mural on the far wall, and under it, a cozy-looking twin bed covered in fluffy pillows and the most gorgeous quilt you have ever seen in your life.

Opposite that is a bookcase crammed with stuffies in all shapes and sizes: cats, dogs, turtles, orangutans, and most important, Ursula, my unicorn. With her big, violet eyes, her swirly rainbow-striped horn, and her white fluffy fur, Ursula was my favorite.

But it's not the furniture or the decorations that truly shock me, the details of my room preserved as if I've stepped into a life-sized time capsule. It's the two eight-year-old girls on the floor making friendship bracelets. Marley Winters and Ellie Charles.

Yes, that's right. Me and my former best friend are there, in the flesh, sitting right in front of me.

My heart is in my throat. I feel ill, and am suddenly desperate to flee, because I have walked smack dab into the middle of that night. That dreadful night I would do anything to forget.

I cannot watch this. Who is this crazy Girl in Black? And why did she bring me here? How did she know? Is she even responsible? Was it her idea? I don't know who else to be mad at, so I will blame her.

Still, as much as I want to close my eyes and look away, I am also curious.

I haven't seen Marley in years, but when I was young, we didn't spend any time apart.

Marley was my best friend. Yet, saying that she was my bestie isn't enough. Marley was more like my sister. We were friends since birth, practically. We lived across the street from each other and our parents were all good friends. Both only children, both girls in a sea of grown-ups, we had each other. Always.

Anyway, all that's history. I don't want to go backward. Things change. Sometimes stuff happens and it's beyond your control.

Why linger on the past? There's no point. And that's when I realize something: Sure, I walked into this soon-to-be-mess by myself, but there is no reason for me to stay here.

I turn around and try to flee, but I can't. It's so stupid! All I have to do is walk back through the beaded curtain, except it's impossible. Physically, I mean.

It was simple enough to walk in through the curtain. I did so without a second thought. But now? Well, this makes no sense. Something is stopping me from moving through it. I can touch the curtain, but it isn't loose or flexible. It is no longer a normal beaded curtain—one that moves and sways. At this point the beads are stiff, and as strong as steel, like prison bars.

I am trapped.

"Hey, Girl in Black? Where'd you go?" I shout. "You told me to follow you and you're not even here, which is so not fair."

"I'll see you later," the Girl in Black replies. Finally! I hear her voice, but I can't tell where it's coming from.

"Where are you?" I scream, frustrated, as I push harder on the curtain bars. This is unbelievable. I am literally imprisoned in a cage of my childhood. "You need to let me out immediately. I can't be here. I don't want to see this."

I hear a laugh from above and then silence. I sense that she is gone.

This is one cruel trick and I don't like it. But I am here, so I turn around. I face the two girls, who are sitting in the middle of the floor. They can't see me and have no idea I'm watching them, of course. It's just like before, back in the gym. This scene is happening in front of me, but I am not a part of it. I am like a ghost, powerless, forced to witness events I cannot control.

I lean against the wall and sink down to a seated position. Hugging my knees, I watch eight-year-old Marley and me. Our hair is in matching braids hanging over our shoulders, both with neat, center parts. Hers is dark brown, almost black, and mine is light brown, but otherwise the same. We always planned stuff like that back then. We are in matching outfits, too. Pink, fuzzy sweaters and jeans with heart patches on the knees. We sewed the heart patches ourselves—learned how to do so in an after-school sewing class.

Marley is teaching Ellie how to do a chevron braid. "Pink and yellow yarn okay with you?" she asks, holding up the two strands.

"Sure," eight-year-old Ellie says. I'll call her EE for short. Her voice is chipper and bright, like she hasn't got a care in the world. And she doesn't—not yet. She has no idea how bad things are about to get.

"Thanks for showing me what to do," EE tells her bestie.

Marley's voice is sweet and gentle as she explains. "Okay, take four pieces of embroidery thread and make sure they are about three feet long. A little shorter is okay, too. Then you fold them in half and make sure that each piece is the same length. After that, make a loop knot at the top to secure everything together. Then, safety pin it to something so it's easier to braid. Do you have a safety pin?"

Her sweetness pierces my heart, makes me ache inside.

"Hold on." Eight-year-old Ellie, I mean EE, jumps up and goes to her dresser. She digs through a drawer and comes back with a safety pin. "How about you pin it to your jeans, like at the knee?"

"Won't that make a hole?" asks Marley.

"Maybe a small one, but it's totally worth it, don't you think?" EE asks.

Marley nods. "Good point." She takes the safety pin and carefully attaches the string and then fastens it to her jeans. "It's V shaped but it's called a chevron braid, I'm not sure why . . ."

She's patient, as usual—generous with her time and talent.

EE scoots closer to her, leans over her shoulder, and squints at the threads.

Curious, open, innocent, and stripped of all armor. No, not stripped. That's not exactly accurate. This is pre-armor. Before I knew I needed it. Before I worked so hard to build it. It makes me want to cry, seeing myself like this, so young and soft. I was someone else completely. A different girl. It's been so long and I've changed so much I hardly recognize myself.

And yet, at the same time I don't want to be here because I know what's coming next. There is nothing I can do to prevent it. I am powerless.

I stand up because my foot is asleep. What a strange thing to be feeling pins and needles, a sensation that happens when your limb is not getting enough blood flow. I guess a lack of blood flow means my blood is still flowing, which means I'm still alive—not exactly a ghost, which has got to be a good sign, right?

Unless this is some new form of torture.

I walk back and forth, stomping my foot to try to

alleviate the weird feeling. I try talking to the girls, crouching down next to them and waving my hands in front of their faces. It doesn't work. Next I try to put my hand on EE's shoulder. I figure if I could move the beaded curtain, maybe I can somehow signal to the girls, as well. Except I can't. My hand goes right through EE's body. Just like before, with my classmates back in the gym.

I could shout for the Girl in Black again, but I sense she won't hear me. Or if she can, she'll ignore me. She obviously likes torturing me. So I give up—I don't have the stamina. I suppose I am here to watch. Wait until I am taken to the next place. Since I don't know anything, I can't plan my next move. And it's insanely frustrating. I hate not being in control.

I sit down on the bed. The soft mattress is familiar. I wonder again if this is all a dream. What if I get under the covers and lay my head down on the pillow and close my eyes? Will I wake up in the present day? In the gym? Or in the hospital? Or maybe in the back of an ambulance?

I realize that none of the above options would be so amazing, but at the same time, each one would be preferable to my childhood bedroom. On this night of all nights.

Now my insides feel twisty, like I'm going to vomit. A small part of me wishes I could vomit on this quilt. Or really, make it disappear.

It's a reminder of simpler times. A past I don't want to think about.

The quilt is gorgeous. My mom made it for me years before when I was stuck in bed for two weeks with the chicken pox. I was feverish and red and itchy all over but most of all, horribly depressed about missing my ballet recital. We were doing *The Nutcracker* and I was supposed to play Clara, the lead part.

It was a dream come true—or would've been, had I not gotten sick.

I had the most beautiful pink leotard with a sheer, silver, shimmery skirt. My mom and I had embedded tiny crystal beads all over the bodice and shoulders. On the night of the dress rehearsal, she'd French-braided my hair, and used more beads there. When I moved, everything caught the light in the most gorgeous way. The real show was going to be amazing.

But that night I felt itchy and feverish and the next day I woke up feeling awful. Worse—there were spots covering my body. My mom rushed me to the emergency room, where the doctor told me I had the chicken pox.

That would've been bad enough, but then the next day I also had an allergic reaction to one of the medications she prescribed. So I felt like I had a stomach virus also, complete with chills and vomiting every hour, on the hour, like I was losing my insides.

My dad was gone—away on a business trip, as usual. But my mom sat by my side. She made me cinnamon toast and brought me fresh water and mopped my forehead with a cool, damp washcloth. She tried to console me as I wept with sadness, curled into a little ball, with tears streaming down my sad, itchy, red, little face.

She told me jokes. She read me books. She sang songs. She cradled me in her strong arms and held me for the longest time, gently rocking me back and forth. But nothing helped. Not until she came up with the idea of making the quilt. She was always so crafty.

The next day she showed me all the fabric swatches she'd gathered. Patches with pictures of my favorite things:

- Shiny, pink ballet slippers, ankle ribbons artfully curled
- A rainbow with fat stripes of color and fluffy white clouds at each end

- A unicorn with a purple-and-white, sparkly horn
- A strawberry ice cream sundae with rainbow sprinkles and three cherries

"Where did you find these?" I marveled.

She smiled but wouldn't give away her secrets. "I have my ways," she replied mysteriously. She made it seem like magic, my mom. I still don't know where she found those patches.

I helped her make that quilt and as we stitched together those squares, I stopped feeling sorry for myself and started feeling better. So I wouldn't be Clara. There was always next year. I had a bright future ahead of me. This was simply a setback, one recital, one Christmas.

The quilt was spectacular. After we arranged the squares, my mom used a sewing machine to put them all together. Then we finished it off with a hand stitch using thick purple thread.

Purple was my favorite color back then—Marley's, too. We had our own club, called each other the Violets. We not only loved the color but the flower, too, and the smell of the violet perfume her grandma, Oma, used to wear.

I'm actually happy to see the quilt—I haven't in years. But that's a different story. Another one I don't want to revisit. Suddenly a guilty lump forms in my throat. I try to gulp it down but can't.

I don't want to think about how sweet my mom is, how soft. I don't want to relive these scenes from my past. Not when I've worked so hard to forget them.

Maybe I should pretend like I'm watching a movie— not of my life, just some random film about some other girl.

If only there were popcorn.

Hey, I wonder if I can get some popcorn. Why not? Nothing else makes sense in this magical universe.

"Popcorn please!" I yell into the air.

I hear a distinct, "Hah!"

I grin—just as I thought, the Girl in Black hasn't actually left me. She's simply disappeared. But I won't be fooled. "I thought you were gone," I call up to her.

She doesn't answer.

I turn back to my eight-year-old self, back to EE.

Marley has finished showing EE how to make the chevron braid. EE is working on the yellow and pink one and Marley is setting up her own, looping together strands in blue and black.

"Who's that for?" EE asks.

"This one is for my dad," Marley replies.

"Oh, I think I'll make one for my dad, too," says EE. "Great idea."

I groan and then cover my mouth, but I don't need to. These girls can't hear me. It doesn't matter what I say or do: no point in trying to warn her.

"He'll love it," Marley says enthusiastically.

She has bright blue eyes, and freckles on her face. She is adorable, my best friend. Former best friend, I mean. There is no one like Marley. I knew it then and I still know it now.

"Do you think he'll be surprised?" EE asks.

Marley nods, encouraging me. "Of course."

EE says, "He never wears bracelets, though. I hope he likes it."

"He probably doesn't wear one because he's never had one this nice before," says Marley, always the optimist.

EE nods. This is exactly what she wants to hear. Marley knows this. Both girls believe it to be true. They are so innocent. Nothing bad has ever happened to them.

"When I'm done I'll make one for my mom," says EE.

"And I'll make one for my other dad," says Marley. "We'd better hurry. Christmas is only three days away."

They both work for a bit until EE looks up and says, "What do you think you're getting for Christmas?"

"A new bike, I hope. One with gears and hand brakes," says Marley. "In violet. You hardly ever see violet bikes around, and I don't want my bike to look like everyone else's."

"I asked for a bike, too," EE says, excited.

"Make sure you get a violet one, too," says Marley. "Then we can be twins."

"But I thought you wanted to be the only kid with a violet bicycle," EE reminds her.

Marley shakes her head. "No, I would love it if you got one, Ellie. You're my best friend. I mean everyone else. We're different."

This warms my heart. Eight-year-old me smiles, and thirteen-year-old me smiles, as well. I can't help myself.

"Let's get matching baskets and bells, too," says EE. "And we can make rainbow streamers for the handlebars."

"We can even use this yarn, if we have some left over," Marley says, holding up the pile of thread.

For a brief moment I wonder if maybe this isn't the day. The day everything went wrong. Maybe I can simply kick back and enjoy the scene. Those were good times, when Marley and I were besties. I had a beautiful quilt that my mom and I made ourselves. I've just about convinced myself of this, and am finally ready to relax, when I hear shouts coming from outside the bedroom door.

It's my parents. Well, of course it is. They had to come around and ruin this eventually.

"I have had enough!" my mom yells.

I startle, and so do the girls on the floor.

"You have no idea what it's like in the real world!" my dad shouts back. "You cannot handle it."

A door slams. A dish breaks. Then my mom starts to scream. "I am sick and tired of it, Nick!"

I feel like puking. I wonder: Will anyone hear my retching? And if I do throw up, will the contents of my stomach be invisible, too?

Marley's eyes widen as she looks at EE.

I am so jarred by this I cannot think straight.

I blink and remind myself that I'm dreaming . . . or something.

This has already happened to me.

Nothing will be as bad.

This moment has passed and I survived.

I am awesome and ruthless, the most powerful eighth grader in my whole entire town. I am going to rock high school, too. People fear me. Nothing can penetrate my icy exterior. I'm not rock-solid, because rocks can crack and crumble, wear down over time. I am more like titanium or steel, or a diamond. Yes, I like that better. Diamonds are hard and sparkly and expensive and rare and that's what I want to be. That is who I have become, and it's working.

But all that is ahead of me, in the future. Now I have to watch EE relive this pain and it's agonizing.

Marley bites her bottom lip and asks softly, tentatively, "Is everything okay?"

"Sure," says EE, forcing a smile, obviously fake, straining at the edges. She takes a deep breath. Her bottom lip quivers. Tears fill her eyes but she sniffs them back and sits up straighter. "It's probably the TV. My mom always listens to it too—"

Before she can finish her sentence there's another scream. "You've got to leave me alone. This is too much!"

"What are they watching?" Marley asks, looking toward the door nervously. Is she that innocent, or perhaps such a good friend that she is playing along? I still wonder.

Feeling sick inside, I raise my knees up to my chest and hug them. I press my forehead into my legs and rock back and forth. Strangely, or maybe it's not strange at all, eight-year-old me is doing the same, curled up like a little pill bug. Wishing she could be that small. I remember the feeling.

Suddenly my mom bursts into the room, surprising Marley and Ellie. Her face is red and blotchy, and her eyes are glassy. She's been crying, and her voice sounds strained. There is so much pain in her eyes. She's trying to hold it together, though.

She takes a deep breath before she speaks, blinks a few times. I can tell that she is attempting to sound calm, but her voice wavers. I didn't notice it the first time I witnessed it. But now I know exactly why she sounds so strange: It's the strain of trying to pretend that everything is normal.

"Marley, honey. I think you need to go home," my mom says in the calmest voice she can manage. She's even trying to smile—the corners of her lips pulled back tight.

"No!" EE grabs Marley's arm and pulls her close, clinging to her. "She just got here and we're still making presents. Marley is helping me with something and it's a surprise for you and Daddy. Please, Mommy. You promised we could have a sleepover."

"Another night," says my mom, soft but firm. "I'm sorry, sweetheart. Truly."

EE throws the friendship bracelet to the floor and says, "It's not fair. Why don't you turn the volume down on the television?"

My mom looks at my eight-year-old self, blinking, confused.

"The shouting from the TV. I don't know what you were watching, but it seemed pretty violent." EE glances at Marley. I know what's going on inside Ellie's head. My head. I still remember, even though it's been five years.

Just play along. Come on, Mom. Don't embarrass me even more.

I am pleading silently and my mom finally catches on.

"Right." My mom sighs. "The TV, of course. That's what the shouting was about. Look, I'm sorry, sweeties. It's simply not a good night. I'll explain it all to you later. Marley, we'll do this again soon, okay? Come on. I'll walk you home."

She holds out her hand. My mother smiles but she means business.

Marley stands up dutifully. She looks down at EE and says, "Sorry."

But EE is staring at the ground, pouting because the

playdate is ruined, mortified that her parents fought in front of her best friend.

It isn't fair and she knows it. I do, too.

A minute after I hear the front door close, my dad comes into my room, looking serious and sad and seriously sad. He sits down right next to me, but he doesn't see me. I try to put my hand on his shoulder, but it goes right through his body.

He doesn't even flinch.

I can't communicate with my dad from the past, but I'm still going to try. "Don't do it," I tell him firmly. "Don't do this tonight. You don't have to say the words. No one is making you do this."

He can't hear me. I know this. I can't do anything but watch. My stomach feels twisty and my whole body aches.

He rubs one hand along the top of his head and lets out a long, sad sigh. "Ellie, darling. Come here." He pats the bed next to him.

Eight-year-old Ellie doesn't move. She stands in front of him, stubborn as always.

"Why do you always have to yell at her?" she asks with a pout. Her voice is soft and trembly. She's afraid to ask this question. It's a big deal that she actually does.

She worries her dad will get mad, will yell at her like he yells at her mom. But he doesn't. He seems too defeated.

"Oh, honey. I'm sorry you had to hear that. It's grown-up stuff. You'll understand when you're older. But for now, well, I don't know how to say this so I'll make it short and sweet. I need to leave. I am saying good-bye."

He stands up, all ready to go, as if it's that simple.

"Are you going on a business trip?" EE asks.

He looks at her sadly and shakes his head. "No, I need to go away for a different reason. Your mother and I . . . Well, I'm supposed to wait until she gets back. Supposed to wait until after Christmas, but that's not going to happen. It's too hard," he says. He kisses eight-year-old Ellie on the top of her head. "Tell your mom good-bye. I'll be in touch."

"Wait, you're leaving right now?" EE asks, stunned. "You can't go until Mommy gets back. I'm not allowed to be home alone."

"I can't wait, Ellie. I'm sorry. Your mother is only across the street. You'll be fine. You're old enough. And it's better if I go quietly. For everyone."

I try to protest, but it's no use. He's gone.

EE starts to cry. I'm crying, too. This is awful. I hate it. I try to give her a hug but can't. Of course I can't. My arms move right through her body so I'm hugging myself, and I don't want to be hugging myself. I have armor. I am protected. I don't need affection—not anymore. I've learned to survive without it. EE is the one who is raw. Vulnerable. Eight years old and her whole world has shattered. Her daddy said good-bye three days before Christmas.

She thinks it's a lousy night. She has no idea what this means.

How bad things are about to get.

How her dad isn't saying good-bye for the night, but basically good-bye to fatherhood.

She doesn't realize, but soon she'll know.

I start shouting in her face, hoping something will get through to her. She can't see me or hear me or feel me but maybe if I yell loud enough. Maybe that's why I'm here. To tell her it's going to be okay.

"Don't cry," I say to EE. "You don't need him. You are smart and beautiful and strong and the most popular kid in school. You run every committee that matters. You have all the power and everyone is envious of you. There's nothing to be sad about. So your dad left you. It happens all the time. So many dads have left. Moms, too. You don't have it so bad. You'll be fine. Better than fine—you will be spectacular." I need her to hear these things, but of course she does not. EE is oblivious. Stunned. Lost. A deer-in-the-headlights expression on her face. She doesn't know what hit her.

"What doesn't kill you makes you stronger!" I yell.

These words get stuck in my throat. The meaning of them stops me cold. Because now I am wondering . . .

Am I dead? Did that fall off the ladder kill me?

Is this whole reliving of the most painful memories from my childhood a part of the dying process?

And if so, what exactly am I supposed to do?

Am I on my way to heaven?

Or someplace else?

How am I supposed to figure this whole thing out?

chapter four

I blink and I'm somewhere else. Did I black out? No, it appears I fell asleep on the floor of my old bedroom. Thirteen-year-old me is curled up on the ground, right in the middle of the rug, kind of like a cat. I stand up and stretch, feeling as if I've just awoken from a deep, deep sleep. I think it's the next morning. The sun is shining brightly outside. Rays bounce off the snow, creating a brightness that is almost blinding.

Meanwhile, eight-year-old Ellie is in bed, under her patchwork quilt. Her eyes look red and puffy, and I know why. She cried herself to sleep.

I look around the room and see that the friendship bracelets Marley and EE were working on are still on the floor in a heap of tangled thread—unfinished.

Suddenly we hear a knock and then the door opens. It's my mom. She turns sideways and pushes through the beaded curtain to come inside. I scurry out of the way, not that she'd even feel it if she walked right through me. Not like I would, either, but still. I don't like being reminded of my ghost-like existence. It seriously freaks me out.

So I move to the purple rocking chair in the corner of the room, where I know I'll be safe, and I watch the scene unfold.

My mom is walking slowly, carefully. In one hand she carries a cup of hot cocoa with an island of fluffy whipped cream floating on top. In her other hand, she is balancing a plate of buttered, cinnamon sourdough toast. I can smell it from where I sit, all the way on the other side of the room. My stomach is rumbling and the very fact that I'm hungry seems like a good sign. That must mean I'm still alive, right? Ghosts don't need food, I don't think.

Eight-year-old me is under the covers, sleeping. My mom sits on the edge of the bed, watching. Smiling lovingly down at her sad little daughter—at me.

From this vantage point I feel as if I'm watching a movie. It feels cozy, somehow. No, not somehow. It feels cozy because that's what my mom wanted, so that is how she made it. Last night, my dad walked out of our lives. That would've been sad enough, but my dad happened to walk out of our lives three days before Christmas. What a disaster. But now, the morning after, all is calm. There is no yelling, no screaming, no more slamming of doors or breaking dishes. My mom has swept up the mess. Cleaned the house. Baked our favorite bread. The entire house still smells of it. She's put on a cheerful face, because of me. I didn't notice it the first time around. But now, five years later, I see it and I am touched by what she's trying to do. Trying to make things happy and safe and warm.

"Good morning," my mom says, her voice gentle, careful. "Did you sleep okay, Ellie?"

Eight-year-old me wakes up and rubs her eyes. And then it hits her.

"Where's Daddy?" EE asks, her voice tinged with suspicion. She knows it's not a good morning, despite the morning treat—hot cocoa and breakfast in bed—and despite her mom's smile.

Mom sits down on the edge of my bed. She brushes young Ellie's bangs away from her forehead. "Daddy went away, sweetheart."

"Is he at work?" Ellie asks, oh-so-innocent. Her eyes are crinkled. She stares at her mom carefully. She knows

74

better. Knows things aren't right. But she's pretending or at least hoping that last night wasn't real. Or that she had a terrible nightmare. Or that her dad changed his mind and came back home, that her parents patched things up. She's imagining lots of possibilities, each one better than the reality she is left with.

"Is he?" she asks again. It's clear that her mom doesn't know what to say. She hesitates now, bites her bottom lip, looks down at her fingernails, which are short and ragged from being chewed.

"Not exactly." Mom takes a deep breath. "Honey, last night things didn't go exactly as I had planned and I'm sorry for that. But maybe it's for the best that you found out the truth sooner. I know your father talked to you about this before he left, but I'm not sure what he said, exactly. So I will give you the facts. Your father has moved out of the house. We are getting a divorce."

"What's a divorce?" EE blinks up at her mom.

She's actually never heard the word before. It sounds strange on her tongue. Sharp and hard. Divorce. She says it again, to herself. It rhymes with *force* and it reminds her of the word *divide*. A forceful divide, violent, which makes a lot of sense. Especially when she thinks about life, sometimes, when her dad was around:

The shattered dishes.

The slamming doors.

The screaming and shouting.

If it sounds like divorce and it looks like divorce and it smells like divorce, well, then it must be divorce. No great shocker there. I know this now. But back then, my eight-year-old self was so innocent.

"Oh, Ellie. Mommy and Daddy both love you very much, but we do not love each other the way married people love each other."

"But when is Daddy coming back?" EE asks, louder this time. Thinking her mom must not understand the question.

"He's not coming back here. Not to stay, anyway. Your father and I are going to live in different houses from now on. And you'll get to live with Mommy and with Daddy, on different weeks."

My mom is speaking slowly and carefully. It sounds like she's reading from a script. Maybe she is. Not now. There's no paper in front of her. I mean maybe she had a script that she memorized. These words sound so foreign, so strange. Eight-year-old Ellie is confused and she looks it. This news is terrible, but her mom sounds so chipper. What's up with that?

EE rubs some sleep from her eyes with the frayed cuff of her purple flannel pajama sleeve. She squints and mouths the word *divorce* silently, trying to wrap her head around it, trying to make sense of the meaning of her world, of her new life, of what will never be the same.

Seeing her process it gives me the chills.

"You have no idea," I warn her. But she doesn't hear me. No one does. There is nothing I can do. So what is the point of this?

Am I supposed to feel sorry for myself? Because I do. I was young and weak and naive. There was so much I didn't see, so much I didn't know, could not control, in my very own house, with my very own parents.

Just like now. I do not want to see this. I lived it once already. And ever since then, well, I've worked hard to forget. To shove these memories away. To punch them down, out of the way and out of my mind.

But like bread dough rises, they keep resurfacing. Growing bigger and more powerful.

"I don't understand," EE says.

My mom sighs and looks at me with tears in her eyes. She leans closer and kisses the top of my head. "I'm sorry, sweetheart. It's not about you. I love you so much. So does your father. We both love you more than anything.

That will never change. But the two of us—your dad and me—we can't live together. And this isn't anyone's fault. I'm sorry about the fight. It wasn't supposed to happen this way. You weren't supposed to see us like that. We were supposed to tell you calmly, together, after Christmas. We wanted to make it through the holiday, to give you one more happy Christmas."

"So where's Daddy now?" EE asks.

My mother frowns. She looks off into the distance. What is she thinking, my mom? How much does she know about the future? I'm guessing she can't know much about the fighting, or the court battle. My dad disappearing from our lives and the money disappearing from their bank accounts. Everything emptied out and untraceable. Coming home and taking all his stuff while we were away—me at school, my mom at work. No warning.

But that happens later.

"We're going to stay here and your daddy is moving out of the house," my mom says gently.

I cover my mouth with my hand. This is what I didn't want to see. This is the worst. I bite the insides of my cheeks to keep myself from crying.

"If he loves me, why did he leave on Christmas?" EE asks.

78

"I can't answer that. But it has nothing to do with you," my mom says as she gently rocks EE in her arms.

Yeah, right. I snort.

Suddenly I feel something on my head. A light ping. I look down. It's a kernel of popcorn.

"Very funny," I call to the sky.

More popcorn pings off my shoulder. "I'm not hungry anymore," I try next. "That was ages ago."

But no . . . the Girl in Black seems to take pleasure in torturing me, because suddenly it's raining popcorn.

"Can I at least get an umbrella?" I ask. Except as I'm talking a kernel of popcorn lands in my mouth. It doesn't taste bad, but that doesn't mean I want more. Not like this. The popcorn is coming down fast. It's like an avalanche. More popcorn than I have seen in my whole entire life. It surrounds me, which would normally be an excellent development, but right now? This is too much. It's too crazy. I'm afraid it will bury me. Also, it's butter overload. I can actually feel the grease. Yuck. "What am I supposed to do with this?" I call out to her, because by now the popcorn is up to my knees.

I'm waiting for some sort of sarcastic remark, since I'm the one who asked for the popcorn in the first place. But instead I'm met with silence, which is somehow more irritating. I know the Girl in Black is watching me, mocking me. And the popcorn keeps coming down, harder and faster like butter-flavored hail.

"Stop it!" I say. But I get no reply. And I hate being ignored.

I stand up and try to shake the popcorn off, but it's impossible. I try to dodge the stream but it follows me, like a storm cloud in a cartoon. It is only raining popcorn on me—nowhere else in the room. Soon it's up to my waist. Then my chest. Then my shoulders. I try eating some, because it is delicious, and I am, in fact, hungry. But it's coming too fast. It's up to my chin. Then a pile rises high above my eyes. Just as I feared, I'm now buried in popcorn. I cannot see. And when I breathe I inhale popcorn kernels. Ugh.

Then suddenly it's gone. Every last kernel, even the one that was stuck in my left back molar. No more butter smell, no more grease. I am clean. Now that's thorough.

Phew. I thought I'd never get out of that nightmare.

Except when everything is clear—when I can see again—I realize something terrible. I'm in yet another scene I don't want to relive.

I remember this night all too well. It's an hour past my bedtime and eight-year-old Ellie is packing her suitcase. She takes sweaters, T-shirts, pants, pajamas, socks, and underwear. She also crams in her three favorite stuffies: a rabbit named Roscoe, a dog named Dojo, and Ursula the unicorn. She'd never forget Ursula. She's taking everything that matters to her, and has no plan to come back. After zipping her suitcase closed, she goes to the window and pries it open. She drops her suitcase down first, and then crawls out herself, into the night, jumping down and landing on the ground below. Luckily our house is only one story.

I follow EE out the window and then scramble across the street. I almost get hit by a speeding car, but jump out of the way just in time. I mean, I think I almost got hit. I don't know if I can die if I'm already dead, but I'm not taking any more chances.

I linger behind my eight-year-old self as she knocks on Marley's window. Marley parts her curtains and rubs her eyes. Seeing EE, she smiles and waves. Then she unlocks and opens the window. It takes both hands to shove it open, but she's strong. EE climbs inside, with me close behind her.

Not that these girls realize I'm there, of course.

"What happened?" Marley asks. "I tried calling you last night and all day today, but you haven't answered the phone."

"I know," EE replies tearfully. "My parents are getting a divorce."

"My aunt Ruthie got divorced three times!" Marley says. "She lives in Arizona now, on a ranch with five horses."

Clearly Marley is not understanding the significance of this moment. How sad and serious it is. It's not Marley's fault, but I'm frustrated nonetheless. I see my younger self struggle to try to explain, which is especially hard since EE doesn't completely get what's going on, either. Not exactly.

EE wipes her nose with the back of her hand. "My dad is gone. He left."

"Where'd he go?" she asks.

"I don't know," EE says, rubbing her eyes. "He didn't say."

Suddenly someone comes into the room. It's Joe, one of Marley's dads—the blond one with glasses and freckles. The one who has a bakery at the mall and always smells like cinnamon. When I was younger I thought his freckles were cinnamon, actually. And I tried to sprinkle cinnamon on my own face so I would match, but it didn't work. Instead I got some in my eyes and it stung really badly. My mother thought it was the cutest thing and told the story all the time until I told her it was embarrassing and she wasn't allowed to mention it ever again.

Anyway, Joe always brings home whatever is a day old and doesn't sell: delicious blueberry bread, chocolate devil's food cupcakes, s'mores-flavored cookies, sour cream coffee cake. The mistakes, too—like the birthday cake that read HAPPY BIRTHDAY, STEVEN when the client spelled his name with a *ph* instead of a *v*.

"Marley, are you talking to someone?" he asks, looking around. "And why is it so cold in here? Why is your window open? It's snowing outside. You'll catch cold."

As he's walking to the window, he almost trips on EE.

Joe stumbles. Then he freezes. He seems shocked but recovers quickly.

"Oh, Ellie. Hello. It's so late. What are you doing here? Did you . . . Did you climb through the window?"

Too upset to speak, EE simply nods.

"But why?" Joe asks.

And that's it. She loses it. EE starts to bawl. It's a big ugly cry. Her eyes are red and squinty, her nose runny.

Joe looks to Marley, confused. "What happened?" he asks.

"Her dad is gone," Marley tells him. "Her parents are getting a divorce."

I am annoyed. I never told her it was a secret, but that doesn't mean she has to blurt it out. Like there's something wrong with me.

Joe actually gasps. "Oh no," he says, moving closer and giving EE a hug. "I'm sorry things aren't great at home right now. You can stay here for as long as you'd like, but I need to call your mom. She must be so worried about you, if she even knows you are gone. I need to let her know, to tell her you are okay."

EE buries her face in Joe's shoulder. She is the last thing from okay.

"Don't call my mom. She'll come get me," Ellie cries.

"Maybe she'll let you stay," Joe says, patting my shoulder. "I don't want her to worry about you. I'll be right back. Okay?" Joe heads out of the room.

Now that the girls are alone again, Marley turns to EE and asks, "Want to make some friendship bracelets?"

EE shakes her head no. "We never finished the last batch. Plus, I don't want to make one for my dad anymore. I can't. I wouldn't know how to get it to him."

"Hmm." Marley frowns and thinks and scratches her head. "Good point. And I think we left all that yarn at your house, but we can draw stuff. I just got some new markers. The scented kind?"

EE sniffs and wipes her red nose. "Okay."

The two girls get to work.

A few minutes later, Joe comes back into Marley's room. "Your mom says you can sleep over if you want to. She'll be by in the morning to pick you up."

"I don't want to go home in the morning. I don't want to go home ever," EE says.

Joe looks at her sadly. "I'm sorry, sweetheart. I know it's rough." He runs his fingers through his hair. "We can figure it out tomorrow. Maybe we can make some crepes. You like crepes, right?"

She sniffs. "Chocolate or banana?"

"Your choice," he tells her.

She wipes her nose with the back of her hand, thinks about this for a few moments before giving her answer. "Chocolate."

"You got it," says Joe. "I'm going to run over to see your mom, get your toothbrush. I'll fill Dave in. He's in the study. If you need anything while I'm gone just ask him. Okay? You girls have a good night."

"Night, Daddy," says Marley. She jumps up and hugs Joe. EE watches sadly.

I know what she's thinking.

I'm thinking the same thing right now. Marley is so lucky I can hardly stand it. She's got two awesome dads. And I've got none.

chapter five

I wonder if maybe I'm in a coma, and if these are simply crazy dreams—flashbacks of painful memories from my childhood still lodged in my psyche like chewing gum stuck to the bottom of my shoe.

I'm probably in the hospital right now. The ambulance must've rushed me here.

My classmates must be so worried about me. I'll bet everyone on the committee is crying. It would be a disaster, me being out of commission today. Any day of course, but especially right now, at this very moment, when I am in charge of this whole, entire night. There are still so many last-minute details to take care of. The rest of my committee could never pull things together in time without me telling them what to do.

And even if they did manage to scrape by, no one would be able to have any fun without me. They'd all be too worried about my well-being. Yes, they must have canceled the dance because of my fall. I am sure of it.

I'll bet everyone is too busy buying me flowers, making me presents, and passing around one of those gigantic get-well-soon cards. My room is probably already decorated with balloons and gift baskets. I'll bet there's so much stuff inside that there's hardly space for the doctors and nurses to fit.

I take a deep breath, thinking that if I can smell the popcorn and the sourdough bread so distinctly, then perhaps I can smell the flowers, too. Except I don't. At the moment, I can't smell anything.

"You really need to get over yourself," the Girl in Black suggests. Her voice booms from somewhere up above.

"Where are you?" I ask, looking around.

The Girl in Black is nowhere to be seen.

I don't like that she can read my mind. It's dangerous, not to mention irritating. Jerk!

"I heard that!" she shouts.

"I know. You were supposed to hear that!" I scream.

I turn back to the scene in front of me. Imagined or not, it looks and feels all too real. Joe and Marley are comforting eight-year-old me, and it is making me sick to my stomach, like physically ill. But how can I feel ill when I'm already in the hospital with a serious head injury? Maybe it's a reaction to whatever medication they are giving me through an IV. I don't know, but one thing I'm sure of—I do not want to see any more of this pathetic scene. I need to leave. I try following Joe out of the room but I can't. The door slams in my face so suddenly, I'm sure Marley and EE will hear it and wonder what's going on. But somehow, the two girls don't even notice.

This is awful.

I turn to face them, and suddenly it's the next day and I'm somewhere else. Still at Marley's house, but now in her living room. So crazy! Sunlight pours in through the window. Marley and I are on the floor of her living room watching some sitcom on Disney Channel.

I remember what I was thinking the first time I watched. How come dads on TV never leave their families? How come everything always seems so funny and cozy and bright? People are full of cheer and everyone always knows exactly what to say. This depiction of family life is the polar opposite of my reality.

Suddenly the doorbell rings. Joe answers, and it's my mom. She's come back to pick up EE.

"I don't want to go," EE says, scowling.

"I know. I'm sorry, sweetie. We have to, though." My mom fidgets, like simply existing is painful for her.

"Stay for dinner," Joe says, stepping close to my mom, warmth and sympathy reflected in his eyes.

"But it's Christmas Eve," my mom replies. "You must be busy."

"It's Christmas Eve, which is our point, exactly," says Dave, coming into the room. He gives my mom a hug. "You should be with loved ones today. Your favorite neighbors."

"Please can we stay for dinner?" EE begs.

"Don't you have family coming?" my mom asks.

"Yes, our parents and my brother and his kids are on their way, but that's no reason to leave. They'd love to see you," Dave says. "Please, don't rush off. Sit down, have a glass of wine. And stay with us. You two are the closest thing we have to family here."

"Well, okay," my mom says, sitting down on the living room couch. Dave joins her and Joe rushes off to the kitchen to get her a drink.

EE and Marley cheer and they grab hands and rush off to Marley's room. They've got stuff to do.

I start to trail them but change my mind. I know

where they are going, what they will talk about. Why not stick around and hear the grown-ups for a change?

"So, how are you?" asks Joe, handing my mom her wine.

She sighs and stares into her glass. "You know," she replies, sounding so defeated.

"I thought you guys were going to wait until after Christmas to tell Ellie about the divorce," Dave says in a low voice.

"That was the plan," my mom says with a shrug. "But you know Nick. He's impulsive. Couldn't wait."

"I'm so sorry," says Joe, now sitting at her other side. "Maybe he'll come back?"

"It's fine. I mean, it's not fine. It's actually terrible. A disaster. But I suppose it was inevitable. I knew the split was going to happen eventually, so why not now? Maybe it's better this way because the worst is over. Rather than agonize over how to break the news to Ellie, well, we've simply ripped the Band-Aid off."

"That's one way of looking at it," Dave says sadly.

My mom nods, bites her bottom lip and starts to tear up. "The thing is, though. I'm scared he's going to ruin Christmas for Ellie forever."

"Ellie will be fine," says Joe. "She's strong and she

has a great head on her shoulders. Plus, she has you as her mom and Marley as her best friend. And us."

My mom smiles, grateful. "You guys are the best. I don't know what we'd do without you."

Suddenly the doorbell rings.

"Oh, that must be your company. We should get going." My mom tries to stand up but Joe puts his hand on her shoulder.

"No," he says gently.

Dave agrees. "We already talked about this. You shouldn't be alone tonight, plus we really want you to stay," he says.

"It's true, and you'll be doing me a huge favor because we have way too much food," says Joe.

"If you are both sure about that," my mom tells them.

"We already set places for you at the dinner table," says Dave.

Joe opens the front door to reveal all four of Marley's grandparents. Marley and EE wander into the living room to say hello. Their hair is in matching French braids and they both have glitter on their cheeks. Marley gives everyone big hugs, and EE stays close to her mom, both of them standing off to the side, watching the reunion and feeling somewhat awkward and out of place. I'd met

Marley's extended family before, a bunch of times, but tonight feels different.

There is cheer and laughter and bustle in this house, and as much as EE wants to enjoy it, she is not in the mood, cannot be a part of it. She feels like an imposter.

Dave's parents go by Oma and Opa and they are from Chicago. Both are roundish with billowy tufts of white hair that remind me of cotton candy. Joe's parents are Fred and Rita. They are tall and skinny and freckly, like Joe, and they are visiting from Toronto. The four of them met at the airport and rented a van. Traffic was bad, Opa informs everyone, but both flights got in on time.

The grandparents peel off their coats. Dave hangs them in the coat closet, one by one.

Opa asks if he can help with anything. Rita pulls a box of chocolates from her purse and says, "I brought dessert."

"Mom, I made three desserts," says Joe. "I told you not to bring anything."

"Well you can never have too much," she replies.

"Oh, wait until you see what's coming," Dave tells her. "It's a feast."

"As it should be," says Oma. "It's Christmas Eve, and our whole family is here together."

I am struck, yet again, at how everyone in Marley's family gets along. They are one big, happy family.

I look to EE, who is watching in awe. I know what she's thinking—I remember. And I'm thinking the same thing right now. Things are never like this in my house. My mom is an only child and both her parents died when I was a baby. I don't even remember them. And my dad isn't close to his family. It's always been just the three of us.

As soon as they get settled, with their luggage in bedrooms, the doorbell rings again and it's Dave's twin brother, Lloyd, his wife, Jenny, and their girls—Alice, who is seventeen, and Annie, who is fifteen. Marley's cousins both have long blond hair and green eyes and cell phones with pink, jewel-encrusted cases. They are confident and self-possessed. It adds up to a glamorous picture. These high school girls impress me. I want to be in their orbit, but I am too shy to actually speak to them.

Everyone gathers around the dinner table. As promised, extra places have been set. I sit down on a folding chair next to Marley.

Oma says, "Ellie, where is your father tonight?"

"Out of town," my mom says quickly.

"On Christmas Eve?" Rita asks. "That's terrible, the

poor man, not able to be with his family tonight. I hope he'll make it back by the morning?"

"It's fine, Mom," Dave says, shooting her a look.

Suddenly awkwardness has enveloped the entire room and it's too much for my eight-year-old self.

"My parents are getting a divorce," EE blurts out.

Her voice isn't even that loud, but everyone hears. I can tell because suddenly there is silence.

"She's right," my mom says with a shrug. Her eyes narrow for the briefest of seconds as she swipes away a tear. She breathes in deeply through her nose and blinks.

"Oh, that's so sad," Oma says, reaching out to my mom and squeezing her arm. "I'm truly sorry, dear."

"Ellie and her mom are strong. Don't worry about them," says Dave. "They'll be great."

No one says anything for a few moments. Everyone simply stares. Even Annie and Alice glance up from their phones to watch. The silence is awkward and horrible. Anything anyone says is awkward and horrible. This whole moment is excruciating with a capital *E*.

Dinner is quiet. Marley tries to joke with EE, but EE is clearly close to tears.

She can't enjoy the ham, the mashed potatoes, the kale salad. She can't even enjoy the amazing desserts that Joe has made: strawberry shortcake, chocolate mousse with fresh berries and homemade whipped cream, and pumpkin cheesecake with a gingersnap crust. He's outdone himself.

"Everything is delicious," says Opa, wiping the corners of his mouth with his napkin. "I am so happy we're here together."

"Me too," says Dave, holding up his glass. "Thank you for joining us, Ellie and Lindsay."

"Thank you. It's been wonderful. But we should get going," says my mom, pushing back her chair.

"No, wait!" says Marley. "We need to open up presents."

"Doesn't that happen in the morning?" asks my mom, panicked, for some reason.

Dave clears his throat. "We have a tradition of opening one gift on Christmas Eve."

"Oh," my mom says, looking uncomfortable.

"But we don't have to," Joe says quickly. "We can wait."

The grown-ups glance at each other meaningfully, but Marley's cousins don't get the message.

"No way. We can't wait!" says Annie.

"You are right. First we crash your Christmas Eve dinner. Then we try to mess with your wonderful tradition. I'll run home and get a present." My mom stands up and smiles wearily. "That's the beauty of living right across the street."

EE claps, little baby claps. Her spirits lift. There's a glimmer of happiness in her eyes for the first time that night.

Watching from the wings, I roll my eyes. "Don't get your hopes up," I mumble, to no avail.

Once my mom is gone, everyone gets up from the dinner table and gathers around the tree.

I follow them there but keep my distance, sitting in the corner with my back up against the wall.

"We don't have to wait," Dave says to his brother.

"Well, okay then." Lloyd heads to the tree and picks out two flat, identically wrapped packages. He hands them to his kids, Alice and Annie.

The girls rip them open and shriek with happiness.

"What is it?" asks Opa.

"New iPads!" they say, cheering and hugging their parents.

Next the grown-ups exchange some gifts. Dave gives Joe a new stand mixer. Joe gives Dave a new laptop. Oma and Opa get each other sweaters. Rita gets a necklace, and she gives her husband a pair of cashmere-lined gloves.

Marley is squirmy with excitement. "It's my turn," she says.

"Well, okay," says Joe. "Why don't you get it, Dave. I'm sure Lindsay will be back any minute with Ellie's."

Dave nods, rushes out of the living room, and comes back a moment later wheeling something in.

It's gigantic. And even though it's wrapped in wrapping paper, it is so obviously a bicycle. The handlebar is poking through so I see that it's violet, just like she wanted.

EE glances at Marley, who is beaming. She leaps off the couch. Tears off the wrapping. It's the most beautiful bicycle in the entire universe. Everyone can see that. Marley even got a heart-shaped bell and a pink wire basket.

"I love it. It's perfect. Thank you. I feel like I'm dreaming," Marley says.

Just then EE's mom comes back inside. She offers EE a flat, rectangular gift wrapped in candy cane stripe–style paper and tied with a big silver bow. EE smiles. Sure, she's a little embarrassed, now being the center of attention. But she's also happy that it's finally her turn.

She tears open the package to reveal an arts and crafts set. Paint, brushes, crayons, colored pencils, and a sharpener. She looks up at her mom, expecting more.

Mom shifts uncomfortably on the couch.

"Um, is that all?" EE asks.

"That's a gorgeous art set, Ellie," Dave says, putting his arm around my mom.

EE looks down at it. Then she looks at Marley's bike. Then back at her measly art set. She is close to tears, but trying hard to bite them back.

Well, of course the art set is beautiful. But not as spectacular as a violet bicycle. EE doesn't even need to say it. No one does, because this fact is so obvious to every single person in the room.

Joe is shaking his head, feeling bad. He didn't mean to upstage my mom. He leans down and whispers to her, "I thought you were going to get the bike, too. I'm sorry, I never would've brought it out."

Except he's too loud, and the room is too quiet, and everyone hears him.

"There's a bicycle?" EE asks hopefully. "Is it violet, too?"

My mom looks like she wants to disappear.

From my spot in the corner, I bury my head in my hands.

Next, my mom bites her bottom lip and stares at me with pity and shakes her head. "I'm so sorry, sweetie. The rest of your presents were hidden in your dad's trunk. And when he left, well, he took his car. I'm sure he didn't realize. I have been trying to call him—that's what took me so long—but he won't pick up."

EE nods, trying to understand. Okay, there's no bike tonight, but who cares. It's dark out. She wouldn't be able to ride, anyway. EE is giving herself a little pep talk, silently in her own head. She's doing her best to keep it together.

EE reconsiders the art set, and then she looks back up at her mom and asks, "Did you get me any paper so I can actually draw stuff?"

Mom sighs and her shoulders slump. Tears spring to her eyes but she sniffs them back in a show of bravery. "I did. I got you three new beautiful pads. But they are also in the trunk."

She hates to disappoint me—I can tell by the agony in her voice. And I hated to be disappointed.

Sure, EE feels bad for her mom, but now she feels even worse for herself. Annie and Alice got iPads. Marley got a bicycle. And what did EE get? A father who disappeared with her best Christmas present? A mom who is now crying in Marley's living room?

What is she supposed to do with one lousy art set and no paper? She tosses it to the ground, and it lands upside down. That's when EE notices that her mom forgot to take off the price tag. The entire set cost $12.99 marked down from $18.99.

"You didn't even spend the full price on my only Christmas gift?" EE asks.

She sounds bratty—I can see that now, clear as day. In fact, I even knew it at the time. But knowing it didn't change anything. I couldn't control myself.

And now I'm witnessing EE unable to control herself.

Her mom tries to calm her down, diffuse the situation. She speaks carefully, slowly. "It's not about how much money I spent. It's the thought that counts. Ellie, I know this is hard. Believe me. But let's focus on the positive. We are healthy. We have each other. And we're making the most of the holiday. I'm sure, eventually, your father will return with the presents. None of this is your fault, sweetheart."

"Why would you even say that? Of course it's not my fault!" EE is not a yeller, but she is yelling now. She can't help it.

Her mom cries harder and this makes EE so sad, and so mad. This whole scene is pathetic. After all, EE is the kid, the one who was wronged on Christmas Eve. So why is her mom the one bawling her eyes out? It's not fair.

"Cut it out!" EE screams, having forgotten that they aren't alone. They are across the street at Marley's, performing in front of her whole family.

Marley with her perfect family. All of them smiling. At least they were. Now they seem horrified. EE can see their shocked expressions.

And it makes her feel like a monster. She has ruined everyone's holiday.

"Your dad will bring you the bike, Ellie." Joe tries to reassure her. "He probably hasn't gotten your mom's messages."

"Right. Maybe his cell phone died, or maybe he lost his phone," Dave adds.

Joe nods, wanting to believe this. "Yes. I'm sure he'll come back with your bike and then everything will—"

"I'm not talking about the bicycle!" EE shouts. Her fists are balled and tears stream down her face. She's hysterical, embarrassed, and ashamed.

I felt it at the time, deep down, underneath the rage. And now I am feeling that shame all over again.

"Please calm down, sweetheart." My mom speaks quietly, looking at the ground. She can't look me in the eye. Is it because she's embarrassed? Because of me or for me? I suppose it doesn't matter.

"How can I calm down? My Christmas is ruined!"

I hate watching this. I'm so sad for my mom. She's suffering. She's in pain. She's a single mom. It's Christmas, and her eight-year-old is acting like a spoiled little brat.

I take a deep breath. I don't want to watch this.

I close my eyes, will myself to be somewhere else. And somehow, I am.

I'm in a dark room with the Girl in Black standing right next to me.

"Why am I here?" I ask.

"You asked to leave," she replies. "You said you couldn't stand to see another moment of that nonsense."

"And now you actually listen to me?"

She shrugs. "What can I say? I was bored, too. You were awful. A monster. I don't want to witness that scene again, either."

"What do you mean, 'again'?" I ask.

She doesn't answer me. Appears to be filing her nails, which are painted bright red. I like the color, but I am not going to ask her where she got it, what it's called. I still have my pride. But I am so curious . . .

More than that, though, I am angry.

"Well, of course I acted horrible," I tell her. "I had just lost my dad, I didn't get a bike, and we were surrounded by Marley's gigantic, perfect family. She had everything, and I had nothing. It wasn't fair."

The Girl in Black isn't responding, which is making me more annoyed. Why doesn't she get it? Do I have to spell it out for her?

"Okay, I was jealous. Is that what you wanted to hear? I was insanely jealous. And how could I not be? Watching Marley's family made me feel more alone. And more pathetic. Marley got everything—perfect parents, cool cousins, four whole grandparents, this big, happy family where everyone gets together for fun holidays, and she even got the violet bicycle with a heart-shaped bell. And me? My heart was breaking, and I got nothing."

"Or maybe you had a lot, but you didn't even see it," says the Girl in Black. "And maybe Marley's life wasn't so perfect. Especially not later. Well, you certainly had a lot to do with that . . ."

"It's not that simple!" I shout.

Rather than answer me, the Girl in Black snaps her fingers and I am back in my room. It's the same night, though.

I can tell because of the quilt.

It's still on my bed.

Not much time has passed. After my big outburst, my mom and I left Marley's.

EE is alone, the art kit in the middle of her bedroom

floor. She opens it up. There are scissors inside and they are sharp.

She looks at the quilt on her bed. She loves that quilt. But she hates it, too, with a blinding, red-hot rage. Her mom worked so hard, with painstaking effort, to sew that quilt, hand stitching each and every square. She did that for EE. Out of love.

But it wasn't enough.

Why didn't she make Dad stay? Why didn't she stop him, put her foot down? Is it because she was too nice? She let him go and for whatever sad, twisted reason, EE blamed her.

And the pain was too much. It overwhelmed her. Made her want to lash out and hurt someone the way she'd been hurt. And the blanket was right there. It seemed to beckon her.

EE picks up the scissors and starts to cut.

She's surprised at how easy it is, how fragile the fabric is. The scissors are sharp and strong, the blades pointy. They glide right through that soft, beautiful fabric.

First EE cuts the quilt in half and then she halves one of the halves. She cuts out each individual square but it's not enough. She has a need to destroy it more. So she cuts through the rainbow. She cuts through the ladybug, the unicorn, and the ballet slippers. She does not stop until she has cut the entire blanket into shreds.

Then, feeling better, she looks at her bed. The faded blue and pink striped sheets underneath. It looks so bare. Stripped of the covering. Not right. Well, it's how she is feeling at the moment—not right. Incomplete, like her new family.

She pushes the pieces into a pile and then scoops them up and throws them into the wastebasket in the corner by her desk.

Then she falls asleep.

When EE wakes up the next morning, her wastebasket is empty. She is draped in a new blanket—one that is plain and blue.

My mom never mentioned the quilt and neither did I. Is that weird? It seemed so at the time. But now it makes perfect sense.

Why *would* we talk about it?

How could we possibly?

There was nothing left to say.

chapter six

I am in the bread tunnel again, running as fast as I can. I pretend I'm in track, doing the four-hundred-meter dash. It's a race I always win handily, and I've got the medals to prove it. I'm thinking maybe I can find the end of this thing, finish my "journey" or whatever it is early, race my way to safety. And I do see some double doors up ahead. They look just like the ones I walked through when this nightmare began. So I push them open and walk on through and find myself in the school gym.

Yes! At first I think: *Finally this lousy nightmare is over and I can go back to my hard-earned and much-deserved position as the most awesome eighth grader ever to walk the halls of Lincoln Heights Middle School.* And I hope I have time to take a shower before the dance starts because sourdough perfume is not my aroma of choice.

But now, mere seconds later, I realize I am in a different gym. I'm still at a school dance, but it's not the one I expected to go to tonight.

I have been in this room before, however. I guess that should be obvious by now. The Girl in Black keeps taking me to scenes from my past.

This whole thing is so annoying, but at least we've moved beyond Ellie Charles at age eight. Those were awful times! EE was like a wounded puppy dog: weak, painfully shy, confused, stunned, and heartbroken.

Now I am witnessing myself at age eleven, and a lot has changed. My dad has been gone for years, the divorce finalized long ago. And although it's not ideal, I've found ways to cope. Namely, my stuffed unicorn named Ursula. I couldn't explain it with words, and it always embarrassed me at the time, but she was kind of like a security blanket, I guess. I slept with her and I carried her around, too. No big deal. I didn't take her out at school or anything. But she was always with me—hiding in my backpack. Sometimes when I got stressed out, or lonely, or sad about my dad or whatever, I'd reach down and pet her.

No one knew about Ursula except for Marley. She understood and would never betray my secret.

Anyway, here I am. I'll call this version of myself E@11.

Tonight is the annual Father-Daughter Dance at my elementary school. It started out so fun! Getting ready for the dance seemed like a party in itself. Marley and E@11 went to the mall and picked out matching dresses. They are silky and violet with puffy sleeves and lacy, ruffled skirts. Their shoes are black patent leather and they both have violet ribbons braided into their hair.

The two girls wear matching patent leather purses. At the last minute E@11 stuffed Ursula into hers. The bag bulged in a way that was telling to anyone who knew about her existence, but Marley was the only one who did, and she'd never tell anyone.

Marley never betrayed me.

It's so weird being back in my elementary school. The gym is so much smaller than the middle school gym, but that makes sense because the kids are so much smaller, too. I wander around, past a table set up with rows of juice boxes and bowls of chips and pretzels. Large potted plants are set up at each end. String lights twinkle from above and the rest of the lights are dim. Trendy pop music is playing.

Everyone is decked out in fancy clothes. Most fifth-grade girls wear dresses or skirts and fancy blouses or flowy pants. Some have their hair woven into braids, like Marley and E@11. A few are wearing buns or pigtails, or have simply blown their tresses out, silky and shiny. Dads are freshly shaved. Their faces beam with pride and joy. They wear dark suits, or khakis and blazers, or pressed jeans and shirts and ties.

Other people's dads, that is.

My own father isn't here. He has a business meeting in Taiwan, so he can't attend. It's been three years since he left, and I haven't seen much of him. He's got an important new job that usually gets in the way. If he's not in Taiwan, he's in Bangkok or Dubai or São Paulo or Qatar.

He doesn't go to dance recitals or parent-teacher conferences or school plays, but I don't expect him to. Even when my parents were married, he wasn't the type of dad to show up to stuff like that. He always traveled a ton for work. And now that he's living in another city, three hours' drive away? Well, it's been hard to see each other. But E@11 is used to his absence.

And tonight she's too excited to care that much because she's at the Father-Daughter Dance with Marley and her two dads.

Joe and Dave are the sweetest. In their navy suits and checked shirts—Joe's is lavender and Dave's is blue—they kind of match, too. And they even bought us corsages—a clump of petite, pale pink roses that we wear on our wrists.

It strikes me from the outside how we look like one big happy family. At this point in my life, Marley's dads do seem like family to me and my mom. The five of us spend tons of time together. We have dinner practically every Sunday. And we've invented all sorts of fun traditions: pizza night on Tuesdays, game nights every other Thursday or whenever we happen to be free and have a hankering to play Monopoly, Sorry!, or Clue. Sometimes Marley and I help Joe in his bakery. He's teaching us how to decorate birthday cakes. I'm really good at making frosting-roses. Cake calligraphy is harder than it looks, but I am making progress.

The four of us have just arrived and we are wandering around, taking everything in. I trail behind them, invisible to everyone.

When an old Amy Winehouse song comes on, Marley says, "I love this song."

"Me too," E@11 replies.

"Well, then we'd better dance," Dave says. He offers

his hand to Marley, and she takes it. They go out into the middle of the dance floor, and Joe leans over to E@11 and asks, "Shall we join them?"

E@11 nods, smiling. "Sure," she says.

I stand right next to them, so I can hear their conversation. E@11 closes her eyes and sways along with the music. She is pretending, not for the first time, that Joe and Dave are her dads, too, that this is her regular life and Marley is actually her twin sister.

I laugh to myself, because the old fantasy is so clear in my mind. My mom would fit in there somewhere, too. Maybe we'd buy a bigger house, and the five of us would live together. Why not? We were best friends, a family of our own invention, and isn't that the best kind?

The song ends too soon. "Thank you for this dance," Joe says to E@11 with a slight bow.

E@11 giggles and says, "Thank you."

Then she and Marley trade dance partners. Now it's E@11 and Dave swaying together. He asks her how school is going, how she did on the math test she was stressing about. Who she and Marley ate lunch with. If the cafeteria still served the icky square kind of pizza. He knows more about her day-to-day life than her actual father. E@11 is keenly aware of this. She loves spending time with Dave.

Still, when a fast song comes on, E@11 says she's taking a break.

I remember how I was feeling that night. On the surface I was excited. But a little deeper down, I was self-conscious and shy and afraid that I was going to do something stupid. I was also wishing my dad were there because he never worried about stuff like that. He had this confidence, was so bold and sure of himself. He wasn't afraid of anyone. I admired him and longed for his company. Everyone else's dad managed to show up.

Even though E@11 loves Joe and Dave, she knows they don't belong to her. She's thinking about the difference and starting to get mopey when, just in the nick of time, Marley grabs her hand.

"I'm thirsty. Let's get some juice," she says.

E@11 is relieved to have something to do. They head toward the drinks, and I follow them. They are moving fast but stop so abruptly that I almost run into them.

Ugh! Of course. The Girl in Black has plunged me into another one of those awful memories. I was so excited to see myself dressed up at the dance, I'd forgotten about this moment. But now I have to watch.

Marley and E@11 are standing there frozen, afraid to get too close to the drinks table because the cool and confident popular girls are already there. It's Lily, Harper, Maddie, and their fearless leader, the most intimidating girl of all: Nicky Braun.

Nicky was particularly awe-inspiring because she had moved to town six months ago and somehow, maybe it was her looks or her attitude or the fact that she had the greatest wardrobe that anyone in Lincoln Heights had ever seen, somehow she became more popular than a celebrity. Everyone at school wanted to hang out with her. And it was Lily, Harper, and Maddie who she chose. Well, of course she did.

They were everything, these girls. The opposite of me: loud and brash and bold and comfortable in their own skin. And back when I was eleven, I wanted to be just like them. It's painful watching the desperation on E@11's face. She is shy and nervous, longing to be accepted by these girls, but afraid to get too close. Intimidated. She feels inferior.

E@11 grabs Marley's hand and pulls her behind the giant potted plant at the end of the table. She knows their place: these two nice girls, sweet and innocent and meek.

Nicky and her friends don't notice us. Well, of course

they don't. We are not the kinds of girls they would notice. So that means we are listening in on their conversation. Eavesdropping, if you will. Except that wasn't our intention. All we wanted to do was wait for them to leave so we could get drinks ourselves. Because the sad fact was, we were afraid to exist in the same space.

But guess what? Crazy coincidence, they happened to be talking about us. Well, about our dates, anyway.

Nicky Braun says, "Did you see Marley dancing with her dad before? She's so lucky. He looks so young and he seems so much cooler than all the other dads."

Marley and E@11 lock eyes and raise their eyebrows. They silently giggle behind their hands.

"Wait, which one?" Maddie asks.

"Which one what?" Nicky asks.

"Which dad?" Maddie clarifies. "Marley has two of them."

"No way. I didn't realize," says Nicky, gazing across the gym at Dave and Joe. "And they are both here?"

"Yeah, the other one was dancing with Ellie," Harper tells her.

"Oh right. I guess I thought that was Ellie's dad." Nicky turns to Harper and asks, "Where is Ellie's dad? Does she have one?"

"Not really. Well, she used to but he abandoned them," Harper explains. "That's what I heard my mom say, anyway."

I see E@11's face and it makes me want to cry. She is frozen, numb.

Even though I've been here before, know exactly what to expect, it's hard for me to hear, as well.

"Wait, what's the story there?" asks Nicky, thirsty for gossip. "Fill me in."

Harper smirks and tosses her hair back over her shoulder. "He left Ellie and her mom years ago. I think he was dating his assistant or something? I don't know the details. My mom and Ellie's mom used to hang out a lot, but then my mom had to stop talking to her because she was so depressed all the time."

The other girls laugh.

Marley and E@11 are no longer smiling, obviously. In fact, E@11 looks close to tears. I get all choked up, too. I want to tell my younger self that things are about to change. "Don't stress about Harper—she doesn't matter," I say out loud, even though I know she won't hear me. "Things work out so well for you in the end. You will come into your own. Nicky transfers to some fancy private school. Then you take over her whole group. Those girls are going to worship you, so don't even worry about this moment. Just get through the summer. You will work hard and you will win. Sixth grade is the beginning of the rest of your life. Everything will change and you will rule the school. It's only a few months away."

I want her to hear me, but she doesn't. Well, of course she doesn't.

I turn my attention back to Nicky and her crew. How could anyone be that mean? These girls are laughing at my expense. Based on something that had nothing to do with me. I mean, so what that my parents split up? People get divorced. Sometimes it's messy. Sometimes dads leave and sometimes moms leave. It happens and there's nothing funny about it.

"Seriously, that's gotta suck," says Nicky. "Poor Ellie."

"I know. It's so sweet of Marley and her dads to be that kind to her," Harper points out.

It *is* sweet is what I am thinking both then and now. But why wouldn't they be sweet? They were our closest family friends.

"They must feel sorry for her," says Nicky.

Ugh. I feel ill. This was bad enough the first time around. But now, having to watch E@11 witness this scene? It's excruciating. I can't take it.

I go right up to Nicky and Harper, thinking maybe if I'm loud enough they'll hear me. And even if they don't, well, I need to get this off my chest. I should've told them off the first time around. "Marley is my best friend," I say through gritted teeth. "Her dads are awesome, but there is no pity involved. How dare you even suggest that? It's crazy! Our families were close even before my dad left. I am not some poor, defenseless puppy who got kicked to the curb, someone Marley and her dads graciously took in. I am no charity case. And I resent the implication."

Nicky and I seem to lock eyes, and for the briefest of moments I think I'm getting through. But no—her cold blue eyes burn right through me. It still chills me, her gaze. It still makes me wither and I hate the power she has over me, how meek she makes me feel. Even after all this time. Even after I've changed. I'm no longer that shy and helpless little girl. I am fierce.

I turn back to E@11. She is crumbling, crying, wondering, is that what people think? It's clearly what Nicky, Maddie, Lily, and Harper think. But do other kids feel that way?

She is shaken to the core. Marley is trying to comfort her but she doesn't hear. She's staring straight ahead. Her face is red. Her whole body is trembling. And she cannot take it for one more second.

Suddenly she is clutching Ursula. Except Ursula is

not in the bag anymore. She is out, in full view. At the dance. E@11 is stroking her stuffed unicorn in front of the most popular girls in school. It's like she's in a trance. She's trying to calm down. But she doesn't realize these girls see her. And laugh.

Actually, they are hysterical and pointing. "Oh my gosh. You brought a stuffie? How adorable!" Harper says patronizingly.

Eventually E@11 snaps out of her fog. She looks at the laughing girls and then down at Ursula. As everything registers her eyes get wide and panicky. Then she drops her stuffie and bursts into tears and runs out of the gym.

I find this heart-shattering.

Meanwhile, the cool girls shrug and go back to their snacks.

But Marley isn't going to let them get away with this. She picks up Ursula, brushes her off, and shoves the stuffie into her own bag. Then she walks right up to them and says, "Ellie is not only my best friend. She is a part of my family. Also, she is amazing and we love her. I could go on and on and on about how wrong you are, but you are not even worth the effort."

Then she turns around and leaves the gym.

chapter seven

Next thing I know, I'm in the middle of a snowstorm. The ground beneath my feet is white and fluffy. Snowflakes float and flutter gently around me. It's pretty in here, but something is off. The entire scene seems too perfect, too self-contained, and somehow, completely artificial. I should be feeling cold, but I'm not chilly in the slightest. And the snow that surrounds me is so sparkly it looks more like glitter. Taking a closer look I realize why. The snow *is* glitter.

Wait a second . . . It seems I am not in the middle of a snowstorm. I am two inches tall and trapped in the middle of the snow globe perched on top of a bookshelf in the public library.

I peer out through the plexiglass and see a younger version of myself at a library table with a stack of books nearby. I'm reading carefully and taking notes. It's the summer before middle school. I remember those months well. I'm still E@11, but in the process of becoming someone else.

Let me explain: Ever since the Father-Daughter Dance/humiliation-fest I knew things had to change. It was a wake-up call. I didn't want to spend my life being pitied, fleeing rooms in tearful hysterics, wishing I'd stood up for myself but not knowing how to. Being too shy to get myself an apple juice when the cool kids were in proximity. Carrying around my stuffed unicorn as a safety blanket. It all made me feel so incredibly weak and pathetic. It's not who I wanted to be.

I saw middle school as a chance to reinvent myself. At my new school, I refused to be seen as the poor girl whose dad left her. I promised myself that things would be different. I would start over, become a completely different person.

All I needed to do was figure out how to make that happen. Always a good student, I knew how to study, so that's where I began—the library. I took the bus there a few times a week, all summer long.

I had plenty of time, too. Marley's dads shipped her off to overnight camp in Wisconsin. It was their family tradition—her cool cousins, Alice and Annie, were counselors. I wanted to go, too, but my mom couldn't afford to send me and my dad refused to. That meant I was stuck at home alone. But I used my time wisely.

I read tons of books about the mean girl cliques and I adopted their techniques. Sure, most of these books were written as cautionary tales, how-to guides aimed at parents worried about queen bee behavior. Titles like: *When Your Child Falls into the Wrong Crowd*, *Helping Victims of Bullies*, and *Combating Mean Girl Behavior*. But I treated them like how-to manuals. That's how I learned about the cruel ruthlessness that separated mean girls from the fray.

And not only did I take notes, I made flashcards. I'm watching E@11 do so now, but why do I need to see this?

"What is the point of this?" I ask, looking around the library for evidence of the Girl in Black. When she doesn't respond, I start pounding on the plexiglass. The glittery faux-snow around me stirs, but the barrier does not break.

"Watching someone study in the library is not exactly my idea of a good time," I call out.

She doesn't answer, but in the blink of an eye, I'm back in my bedroom. I've grown a little bit, in that I'm not tiny enough to fit in the snow globe. Now I'm the size of my stuffies, and on my bookshelf, wedged between my lion and pig. Ursula is long gone—as much as it pained me, I threw her in the garbage soon after Marley returned her to me. But I don't want to linger on those thoughts.

From this vantage point I can watch my eleven-year-old self at work.

E@11 has got her laptop on her lap. She's watching a teen movie, one about a cheerleading competition. Actually, that's not exactly accurate. She's watching one pivotal scene of the cheerleading competition movie: the part where the head cheerleader is yelling at the rest of her squad to get into shape. E@11 pauses the scene, scrolls back to the beginning, and watches it again. When it concludes, she scrolls back again. And again, and again, until she has the cheerleader's words memorized, can recite them along with the scene. It's intense.

Next thing I know, we're at the mall. I'm trailing behind E@11, who isn't shopping. This is a reconnaissance mission. One of many she took that summer. E@11 is in disguise, wearing a bowler hat and sunglasses. She's following around some cool-looking high school girls. She wants to know how they talk and dress and walk and how they do their hair.

I remember it all too well. That afternoon, I went home and practiced my *withering glare* in the mirror until I gave myself the chills.

That first day of middle school, I was ready. I had my arsenal: perfect hair, a trendy outfit, trademark phrases, a distinct strut, and, perhaps most important, a killer attitude. I pretended to be above it all, better than everyone around me. And the meaner and more manipulative and intimidating I acted, the more people I was able to draw in. It sounds weird, counterintuitive, but it totally worked. I'm living proof. Everyone fell for my act. It was all so much easier than I had imagined.

There was only one sticking point, a holdover from my former life: Marley Winters.

I remember the moment she came home from camp, sunburned, with bug bites dotting her legs, and dressed in this old, ripped T-shirt and khaki shorts. She looked relaxed, and happy, and so very Marley.

We hugged and I said, "Oh, Marley. You must change immediately. Khaki is so ten years ago. Have you looked in the mirror?"

"Um, there were no mirrors at camp," she told me. "And I bought these shorts three months ago. They're practically new."

She was hopeless.

As soon as I have that thought, I'm transported again. In the blink of an eye I'm inside Marley's old fish tank, floating around the surface on a raft and wearing my favorite pink bikini.

"Nice touch, Girl in Black," I call out, with no idea if she will respond or even hear me.

"What can I say? You have inspired some of my best work," she replies instantly. "This job is too fun."

I look around but can't spot the Girl in Black anywhere. "So it's a job, being tour guide of my life? That means someone hired you, right? Who might that be?" I wonder out loud. "Or are you self-employed? Please tell me more. I'm fascinated."

Silence. She's gone again, leaving me alone, excluding Marley's goldfish, Bob, and Myrna, her mermaid. But they don't count, obviously, because they can't even talk and one of them is plastic.

I do hear voices, though. It's Marley and me. I'm still E@11, but by now my transformation is nearly complete. I can tell by my outfit. I'm in designer jeans and a fluffy sweater, and I'm wearing tinted glasses even though we are inside and my vision is perfect. I look like an entirely different kid and I'm acting like a different kid, too. My image has been carefully constructed.

Both E@11 and Marley are giggling like crazy, high on sugar, having just eaten three cupcakes each, rejects from the bakery. They were supposed to be frosted purple, but someone in the kitchen added too much red to the blue and the result was brownish. No one wants brown frosting unless it is actually chocolate flavored. Otherwise, it's a total disconnect. This is what Joe has explained to us, anyway.

"So tell me again about your birthday," Marley says.

"Okay, here's the plan," E@11 says. "I'm inviting you and Harper and Maddie, but not Lily."

"But I thought we liked Lily," Marley says.

"We do," I say. "But we can't include everyone because then there'd be no drama."

"And that would be bad?" asks Marley. "You're saying you actually want the drama?"

"Yes, of course," E@11 explains. "Otherwise, we'll be bored because there won't be anything to talk about. Here is the trick: You invite all your besties except for one. This will leave her feeling lost and confused and jealous and most important, desperate to please. She'll be super vulnerable and feeling weak and that's when we strike. We'll freeze her out. It'll be great."

"But why would you do that?" Marley asks, innocent as always.

E@11 stares at Marley pointedly. "What do you mean why? Because we can—because it'll be fun to watch her squirm."

"So you want us to go out of our way to hurt Lily's feelings when we're supposed to be friends with her now? Are you saying it's like a sport?" asks Marley.

E@11 stares. Her smile wobbles ever so slightly. I remember what I was thinking: I wanted to remind Marley about the Father-Daughter Dance.

She was there, too, hiding right next to me. Does she not remember how pathetic it was? She saw me cry. She witnessed my pain and heartbreak.

But I don't say any of that. To be honest, I'm disappointed that Marley would need an explanation. It made me question our friendship—how well she knew me.

"It's more like a hobby," E@11 replies.

"Manipulating people's emotions seems like a weird hobby," Marley points out.

"I'm only having fun," E@11 replies.

Marley looks down at the ground. "I don't think that's my idea of fun," she says.

"Well, then you don't have to come to my birthday. Maybe I should invite Lily instead of you."

"I never said that," Marley says. She's so steady, so reasonable. I find this irritating, too. It feels like a personal rejection. I'm suddenly all too aware of the fact that Marley doesn't need to jump through these hoops. It's like we both know she's better than me, but neither of us is going to say so.

The girls are silent for a bit. I remember how awkward I felt that afternoon, how I tried to explain my logic. "Anyway, Lily needs to be taught a lesson. She thinks she's so great, but she's not. She's addicted to chocolate, and I hate her new boots. They are so pointy. They remind me of witch shoes," E@11 says.

Marley blinks and cringes, surprised by my harshness. "I didn't notice."

"Were you too distracted because of Harper's total pizza face?" E@11 laughs.

Marley doesn't.

"What?" E@11 asks, because Marley is supposed to laugh. She's being funny.

But instead Marley fidgets and bites her thumbnail

nervously. Finally she says, "Everyone gets acne some-times. And no one can help it. I don't think it's nice to make fun of her for it, and I'm confused because you worked so hard to be friends with all these girls, so why are you saying so many mean things about them behind their backs?"

E@11 doesn't say anything in reply. She's frustrated, uncomfortable, and a little embarrassed. Why can't Mar-ley go along with the plan and stop asking silly questions? Why does she have to overthink everything?

I remember exactly how I felt back then and I feel the same way now. Even though I'm two inches tall and in a fish tank, these feelings are still there, and they are big and I hate having them. And I shouldn't have to explain— not to my best friend, who should know better. If I'm not the bully, then I risk being bullied. I'm that sad girl again, crying at the Father-Daughter Dance. The target. The one to be pitied.

It's taken a lot of effort to get to where I've gotten, and I'm not about to throw it all away over somebody's stupid hurt feelings.

"I'm just kidding," E@11 says finally, because she has to say something.

"I know you are deep down, but you make these

jokes and they aren't always funny," Marley says. She's right. They aren't supposed to be funny. They are supposed to cut people down. So I can be more popular. So people will fear and respect me. What did kindness ever get anyone?

"Let's talk about boys," E@11 says, needing to change the subject.

"Okay, what about them?" asks Marley. She doesn't know where E@11 is going with this but she is open-minded, trusting.

My heart twinges with guilt.

"If you were stranded on a desert island with one boy, who would it be?" asks E@11. She's lifted this question from a teen magazine she'd recently studied, and was excited that she finally had the chance to ask someone for real.

Marley thinks about this for a moment. "Why would I be stranded on a desert island?"

This is so Marley. She's not supposed to question the question—she's simply supposed to answer it. "I don't know. Maybe we're on a class trip and our boat crashes into an iceberg and you two are the only ones who survive."

Marley frowns as she puzzles over these facts. "How

would we take a class trip to iceberg-infested waters? I don't think the PTA has the budget to send us to Antarctica or Patagonia. Or, I wonder, where else can you see icebergs? Should we look it up?"

"No, I don't want to look stuff up. That's not the point of this."

"But you were talking about icebergs," says Marley, oh-so-innocent.

"This isn't about icebergs," E@11 says. "It's about the island. So use your imagination."

"Okay. I'll try." Marley crosses her legs and closes her eyes and tries to concentrate. Soon, though, she opens them again and asks, "Um, how long are we on the island?"

"Does it matter?" asks E@11 impatiently.

"Well of course it does. If it's a short time, no big deal. But if it's more like a few days, well, I want someone I can talk to so I don't get bored, someone who could keep me warm if I'm cold. Oh, I know!" Marley snaps her fingers, excited, and then she says, "Eli Delphy."

"Eli Delphy?" E@11 asks, shocked because Marley has named the geekiest guy in school.

She nods. "Yes. He's an Eagle Scout and goes camping all the time, so he must have excellent wilderness survival skills. And you know what he told me once? He knows how to make a fire out of two sticks. And he wears glasses, so in a pinch I'll bet he could use them to harness the power of the sun."

"Huh?" E@11 is so confused. It's truly mind-boggling.

Marley tries to explain. "You know—he could train a lens on a bunch of dry leaves. Make a nice warm fire. Unless his glasses fell during the crash into the iceberg, or slipped off his face while he was swimming to shore."

"What are you talking about?" E@11 asks.

"You are right. I'm overthinking this. Let's go with Eli keeping his glasses. And hey, are there marshmallows on the boat? Can they wash up onshore, as well? They float on hot chocolate so they'd probably float in the ocean, right? In fact, that would be even better because if the water was iceberg infested then it must be cold, so the marshmallows wouldn't melt. I wonder if they'd freeze, though. Do you know? Hey, want to put marshmallows in the freezer and see what happens?"

I roll my eyes. "That's not what I meant and I do not want to do food experiments right now—that's for little kids."

"No it's not," Marley says, frowning.

"Well, we're in the middle of something else and you

didn't answer the question the right way. You weren't supposed to tell me who you think would be the most practical. You're supposed to tell me who you like."

"Oh sorry, you didn't say that. I like a lot of people," Marley tells me.

E@11 rolls her eyes. It's something she's been doing with more frequency, whenever she spends time with Marley, come to think of it. E@11 has been wondering, is her best friend really this innocent? It's hard to tell.

Things are off. E@11 is changing. And she wants her best friend to change right along with her. Otherwise it's lonely. She doesn't want to leave Marley behind. And she doesn't want to get left behind herself.

"I mean who do you have a crush on? Like, what boy?"

"Oh," Marley says, nodding. "I get it now. Sorry."

"Well . . ." E@11 isn't going to let this go.

"I don't know if I want to be on an island with someone I have a crush on. It could get awkward."

"What do you mean? Why would it get awkward? Wouldn't it be awesome to be with the person you're crushing on, just the two of you with no distractions?"

"Nope," says Marley, shaking her head decisively. "Think about it. For one thing, I assume I wouldn't have my toothbrush on this island."

"Um, I didn't really think about that but you are right—a toothbrush would not wash up onshore and there's definitely no pharmacy or whatever on the deserted island."

"Okay, so that means this is a person I would have to talk to with morning breath all the time. And he'd have morning breath, too. It's one thing to like someone at school. Someone who is freshly showered and has combed his hair in the morning and washed his face, and like I said, brushed his teeth, but to like someone enough that you want to hang out with them stripped of that? I'm going to have to think about it."

"Ugh!" E@11 groans and smacks her palm to her forehead. "I give up," she says.

Marley giggles. "What? Do you expect me to act totally boy crazy and ridiculous? Like, OMG I have the biggest crush on Luke Watson? I love his British accent, and how he parts his hair in the middle and wears argyle socks, like, every single day."

"Really?" E@11 asks, perking up. "I had no idea."

"I'm kidding," says Marley. "I know you want me to be all boy crazy like you and Maddie and Harper and Lily, but it's not going to happen. It's not who I am."

This is amazing. She's so self-assured. Knows exactly who she is. At the age of eleven, everything was in flux for me. I was still figuring out who I was and who I wanted to be. That was the difference. That's what was so confounding about Marley. Marley knew exactly who she was and was brave enough to be that person. It was yet another thing that made me so jealous of her.

Still, we had so much history. And she was so good. And so fun.

Suddenly Marley gives E@11 a sly grin and says, "Unless I'm pretending . . ."

She jumps up and heads for her laptop, where she puts on "Crazy for You," the old Madonna song. Then she starts dancing, all silly and ridiculous. Her whole body wiggles like she's a piece of cooked spaghetti. Next, she struts across the room, hips sashaying, like she's on a catwalk. "I, Marley Winters, on this night in December, do hereby acknowledge that I have a huge crush on Toby Benson."

E@11 laughs and says, "Come on, don't make this into a joke."

"I'm not. I'm totally serious. I do," Marley replies. This news is outlandish. Toby Benson is a total geek who plays the cello and chews with his mouth open. He tried to start a chess club at our school but no one wanted to join. He is a loser with a capital *L*.

Marley raises her finger to E@11's lips. "I haven't told anyone. Please keep it a secret, okay?"

"Are you making fun of me?" asks E@11.

"Maybe, maybe not," Marley says coyly.

She's having fun, dancing like she's never danced before. Her face is contorting into crazy expressions.

"Wait, this is too good. I need to get this on video," E@11 says as she pulls out her phone.

Marley puts her hands in front of her face. "I never said you could record this!"

"Come on, it'll be fun," E@11 says. For the moment, it feels like old times. She and Marley just being silly together, acting goofy and making each other giggle. "And no one else will ever see it. It's just for us. Let's make the most ridiculous videos we can. You go first and then I'll do the same."

"I don't know . . ." Marley bites her bottom lip, unsure.

"We'll delete them after we watch," E@11 promises.

She means it, sincerely. I know she does. E@11 loves Marley. Sure, she gets annoyed with her sometimes, feels slightly misunderstood, wishes they had more in common these days and worries that they are drifting apart. But she wouldn't ever do Marley any harm. Not intentionally, that is. The whole thing was a mistake.

If I knew back then what was going to happen, well, I never would've pulled out my phone.

From the fish tank, I gulp with guilt. Wishing I could put a stop to this but knowing I'm powerless—it's a horrible feeling.

"Fine!" Marley says.

She rolls her eyes and then continues strutting around her room. She grabs a red plastic hairbrush and sings into it as if it is a microphone.

"I love you, Toby!" Marley yells. "I think about you all the time. I'm, like, a total stalker. I followed you to class. I am only in the French Club because of you. I made my dad teach me how to make croissants and I don't even like croissants. Or berets. I should be taking Spanish. But no, you take French, so I take French. At night, when I go to sleep, I don't count sheep. I count Tobys jumping over hurdles. One Toby. Two Tobys. Three Tobys. Four."

Arms splayed like some clumsy bird, Marley leaps across her bedroom as she gushes on and on and on. It is a ridiculous spectacle. And she's not even done yet. "I am going crazy for Toby. And guess what? I also kind of like Jett. Jett, with his shoulder-length hair and big brown eyes and the blue ski cap he wears almost every single day. He's adorable. And then there's Beckett. He posted this video of himself snowboarding and I've watched it, like, a hundred times. I'm obsessed. With all of them, I mean. I am basically boy crazy."

She shakes her hips and wiggles her head around on her neck. She is doing the boy-crazy dance—something she invented on the spot. It cannot be more ridiculous and entertaining. And it is *so* not Marley. Somehow this makes it even more funny. It's like she's breaking out of her skin, going wild and crazy.

E@11 laughs so hard that she is trembling. She can barely hold her phone straight for the shot.

The song ends but Marley is nowhere near done with her performance. She starts singing her own tune. Making up crazy lyrics.

She's in her own world, does not even seem to notice that E@11 is still filming this and egging her on. "Go Marley, go Marley, go Marley, go Marley," E@11 chants to the beat of her song. But Marley has more to say. She looks directly at the camera and goes, "I have never kissed a boy, but sometimes at night I practice by kissing my old American Girl doll. I cut the hair off so she looks like a boy. Okay. I'm done. No, not really."

Marley lets out a belch. "I burp all the time. I feel so silly. It's great to confess."

E@11 says, "More, more, more."

Marley shakes her head and wipes some sweat off her brow with the back of her hand. "Cut!" she says. "That's everything I've got."

E@11 finally turns off the camera. Marley collapses to the ground like a windup toy that's finally out of juice.

"That was spectacular!" E@11 says. "I'm so impressed."

"It was fun," Marley says between pants of breath. "Let's see how I did." She comes around so she can see the phone. E@11 and Marley play the video back and crack up because it's so ridiculous.

They watch it a second and then a third time and then Marley goes, "Okay, it's your turn now."

E@11 shakes her head. "Oh, I don't think I can top that."

"Well, you've got to at least try," Marley insists.

Except, before E@11 has a chance to perform, Marley's dad Joe knocks and then opens the door. "Honey, your guitar teacher is here. Ellie is going to have to go."

"But, Dad, we're in the middle of something," Marley argues.

Joe shakes his head. "He gets paid by the hour, sweetheart. I'm not going to let him stand around. Let's go."

"Fine," she says with a melodramatic sigh as she

grabs her guitar from the stand next to her desk. Turning to me she says, "You are up next time."

"Definitely. I'll practice my moves at home," E@11 says, standing up and sliding her phone into her back pocket.

E@11 lets herself out and I'm right behind her, and no longer two inches tall or in a bikini. This time I don't even ask—I'm used to all the crazy transitions and I know my job.

I follow E@11 home in silence.

"Hi, sweetheart," I hear my mom say as soon as we walk through the front door. "You girls have fun this afternoon?"

"Sure," E@11 says.

"You didn't happen to do your homework over there, did you?" Mom asks.

"No, I'll go do it now," E@11 says with a groan as she continues to her room.

She unzips her backpack and pulls out her planner, sees she has a few pages in math and then two chapters to read for history. She starts the math but soon grows bored. She checks her phone. No calls. No texts. She tries calling her dad, but the phone goes straight to voice mail. She doesn't leave a message but texts, *Call me*, knowing that he won't.

E@11 hasn't seen her dad in a few months and this annoys her, but she doesn't want to think about it so she goes back to the video and watches Marley again. It's so funny, she is laughing out loud. It's cheering her up. And she needs cheering up. This is the time of night when, years ago, E@11's dad would come home and the three of them would eat dinner together. She misses those days.

Just then there's a knock on the door and her mom says, "Sweetheart, I'm making some bread. Would you like to help?"

"No thanks," E@11 replies.

She doesn't want to be around her mom when she's upset. Her mom will ask her what's wrong and she doesn't want to talk about it. What's wrong is that she's jealous of her best friend, who knows exactly who she is, and doesn't care what other people think. This makes E@11 feel even more inferior than usual. What's wrong is she misses her dad and she's mad that he's ignoring her calls. She could put on a cheerful face but her mom would see through it. Her mom notices everything. E@11 doesn't want to upset her. Doesn't want to grow more upset herself by sharing her feelings.

Better to be alone in her room. Steely and strong, looking at videos. Texting her friends. Let her mom make the bread. It wasn't E@11's idea. The whole starting-from-the-same-starter is her mom's tradition from a drastically different time. Carrying on with it almost feels false, because they don't have a big happy family and it's dumb to pretend like they do, like nothing has changed. Everything has changed and no one asked E@11 what she wanted. The way life turned out, she and her mom alone, none of it was her doing. She shouldn't be forced to make bread. Also, ugh! She doesn't want to think about any of that, so she looks at her phone again.

She decides to send Marley's funny video to Maddie. Then, when Maddie doesn't respond right away, she sends it to Harper and Lily.

Lily texts back almost immediately: *OMG—crazy Marley!*

I know, E@11 texts back.

"How's that homework coming?" her mom asks, poking her head into the room.

"I'm halfway done," E@11 says without looking up from her screen.

"Glad to hear it," her mom says. "Want me to take your phone so you don't have the distraction?"

"No, that's okay." E@11 makes a show of turning off her phone and tucking it into the drawer of her bedside table. Then she cracks open her books. Later on, after she finishes, it's time for dinner: delicious roasted chicken and salad and bread that she doesn't want to enjoy but has to admit is wonderful.

She forgets all about Marley's silly video, until the next day.

"I only sent it to three people!" I shout.

"But you promised to delete it," the Girl in Black says. "That was the deal."

"It's not my fault it got forwarded," I insist.

"Do you really believe that?" the Girl in Black asks me.

And I can't argue with her. I feel too guilty. I don't need to see what happened next because it's something I'll never forget. That video spread like wildfire. By the time Monday rolled around, it seemed as if the entire school had seen it.

chapter eight

Next thing I know, I'm in the girls' bathroom watching Harper, Maddie, Lily, and E@11.

Lily is eating M&M's, sneaking them out of her pocket. Harper applies mascara. Maddie touches up her lipstick. E@11 looks at herself in the mirror. And of course, like the rest of school, all they can talk about is the video.

"OMG, if that was me I would die from the humiliation," says Harper.

Maddie guffaws. "That dance she did? Do you think she was kidding? Or is that seriously how she moves?"

"The girl has no rhythm," Lily says, as she wipes her mouth with the back of her hand.

"You can't even say Marley and rhythm in the same sentence. It's a total disconnect," Harper says.

E@11 bites her bottom lip and looks away. She knows she should defend her friend, but she's scared. She never meant for the video to get out like that. Only sent it to a few friends. At the same time, she knows this is all her fault. But she doesn't want to accept it. She's hoping it'll go away if she ignores it.

"My God, that whole Toby thing? I can't believe it. If that were me, I would literally melt out of humiliation—I'm talking serious puddle on the floor," Maddie says. "I'd never show my face in school again."

It's too much. They have gone too far. It was just a silly game. No one was supposed to see, let alone take it so seriously. E@11 wishes they would just stop talking about it, but she can't tell them that. She can't stand up to her new friends. She's too afraid of losing them. She doesn't know them that well, after all. Her position is too new. Everything feels so precarious, like it could disappear in an instant with one false move.

But she has to say something, so she narrows her eyes at Maddie. "Well, if you're a literal puddle you wouldn't have a face, dummy," E@11 says.

The rest of the girls giggle.

There. She's upset Maddie, made her feel dumb, but hasn't made fun of Marley in the process. It's a win-win. She's doing her best!

Then a toilet flushes. Everyone goes quiet. Somebody else is in the room and she must have heard everything. But who could it be?

E@11 and her posse look at one another with wide eyes.

The lock slides and the door opens with a creak.

E@11 fears the worst. But what are the odds? It could be anyone in that bathroom stall. The chances of it being Marley are minuscule. Except . . . Except it is Marley. Of course it is.

She steps out of the bathroom stall. Her cheeks are flushed and her eyes are red and glassy. She stares straight ahead and walks stiffly to the sinks. E@11 jumps out of the way of Marley as if she's got some highly contagious, flesh-eating disease.

Marley washes her hands and leaves without looking at any of the girls. It is the longest forty-five seconds of E@11's life thus far. E@11 feels like a piece of dirt, but she struggles to appear neutral, cold, steely, and strong.

As soon as she's gone everybody cracks up. Almost everyone. I'm not a monster and I certainly wasn't one in the sixth grade.

In fact, E@11 rushes out of the bathroom and I follow

her. I know that E@11 wants to apologize and that is her plan. But then she sees three seventh graders following Marley and doing her dance and she hesitates.

I remember this moment, cycling through the options in my mind, trying to weigh potential costs and benefits like an accountant with a spreadsheet.

E@11 can defend her best friend, but then those other kids might laugh at her, too. Because the cold, hard facts remain: If E@11 associates herself with a nerdy kid, then she'll be nerdy, too.

She loves Marley. She truly, truly does. And it makes her feel rotten inside.

Still . . . After she's worked so hard to climb to the top, she can't let one stupid video ruin her efforts. Not even when this whole situation is sort of her fault. Not even when she is witnessing her best friend's heart break into a thousand pieces. Marley tries to get away, but these kids are relentless. "Is Toby really the one?" a girl asks.

Another asks, "Which American Girl doll do you like making out with? Kit is my favorite."

And her friend goes, "Let's hear you belch!"

Suddenly these two eighth-grade boys jump in front of Marley and say, "Hey, Marley, we made up this dance and we named it after you."

One of them starts a beatbox, imitating the sounds of

a drum with his mouth. Then the other starts chanting, "The Marley, the Marley, the Marley . . ."

And then they both do this totally awkward and embarrassing dance. They trip and stumble and then they try to right themselves but trip again.

It is horrible, but others find it hilarious. Then, much to my horror, two more kids start doing it. Marley tries to escape, backing slowly away, but the crowd starts to follow her. And then more kids join in.

Soon it becomes a mob scene. Marley is crying. E@11 is crying, as well. And I feel tears streaming down my own face. It's too much. Eventually Marley snaps out of her trance, spins around, and makes a break for it. She's running so fast no one can catch up, and honestly, only a few kids bother to try. More are hunched over laughing and giving one another high fives and fist bumps. This is entertainment in middle school? It's excruciating.

Marley is gone. I don't bother following her. I don't need to.

I remember how I felt back then—what I was worried about. That Marley's dads were going to be so disappointed in me. I figured they would tell my mom the entire story, every last gory detail. The three were so close. And I knew my mom would take Marley's side and refuse to see my point of view. I sure wasn't looking forward to that lecture. My mom would probably make me march over to Marley's house and apologize. Bring her a loaf of sourdough bread or flowers or both.

A big part of me wanted that, to reconcile with Marley. But then I thought about those laughing girls, how I didn't want to be pitied. How hard I'd worked to claw myself out from that hole.

You can't have everything.

I planned the speech I would give my mom, the fit I would throw. "I'm old enough to choose my own friends. You can't control who I hang out with. This has nothing to do with you. So stop trying to micromanage my social life. Dad would never smother me like this . . ."

My mom would be mad. Maybe she'd shout back, remind me of all the good times Marley and I have had over the years. How she's so smart and sweet and wonderful and how easy and nice and lucky it is that I have my best friend living right across the street. How wonderful she and her dads have been since the divorce. How I can't throw everything away, become a different person and forget my old life, my old friends, like a snake sheds its own skin. I am not a snake. I cannot lose the essential part of myself. My history. My starter.

Maybe I secretly wanted my mom to force the issue so I could pretend like I had no choice but to apologize, make amends. I sure thought about it enough.

But she never did.

A few days passed.

And then a few more.

I went to school. I listened to my friends make fun of Marley. I never joined in, but I never stopped them, either. Never stood up to them and defended her.

Eventually people stopped talking about it. Other stuff came up. Mr. Romero, the social studies teacher, had a heart attack and was in the hospital and everyone organized a bake sale to raise money to help with his rehab. Then Grant Sessions fell off his trampoline and broke both of his legs. He had to go to school in a wheelchair. It was exciting.

I could've texted Marley and told her the coast was clear, that everyone had forgotten all about the stupid video and it was safe to come back to school. Because she'd stopped coming, I'd noticed. And I thought about her a lot. Worried like crazy.

But I didn't do anything.

Not even after Marley started texting me.

Ellie, can we talk?

Please?

We really should talk about this.

I ignored her efforts, did not reply even once.

When she tried calling me, I didn't answer the phone.

She knocked on my door a couple of times, as well, but I never answered. My mom did try to get me to the phone once, when she called our landline, but I said I was too busy.

"I'll call her back," I said, not even looking up from my homework.

We both knew it was a lie. I had no intention of calling Marley back.

Come on, Ellie. We need to talk about the video, Marley texted a few days later. Eventually I blocked her number.

And whenever she waved at me from across the street, I pretended like I didn't see her, acted like she didn't exist. I did that to my best friend.

Some weeks later, I started hearing about Marley again. That she wasn't coming back to our school. She'd transferred to a magnet school two towns over. Was it true? Did she transfer schools to avoid me? Or was she too embarrassed to show her face at Lincoln Heights Middle School? Or would she have left anyway? I don't know and I couldn't even ask.

A few months after this whole thing went down, a for-sale sign appeared on her family's front lawn. The house got snapped up quickly, and suddenly Marley and her dads were gone. They only moved a few streets over. At least that's what I overheard my mom tell someone. It's the only way I knew. My mom still got together with Dave and Joe on occasion, but she was always so secretive about it. I never saw any of them again. Marley, either. We never spoke after that day in the bathroom. What was the point? I knew I betrayed her. I knew I was rotten.

Sure it felt strange, like heartbreak. For the longest time I felt like there was something missing in my life. It's like a piece of my heart dissolved, just evaporated into thin air. It's different from the feeling when my father left. That was horrible in another way. My dad's leaving us was beyond my control. I felt helpless, weak. This was something I did. I tried to deny it, told myself otherwise, but I knew.

I made a choice.

This was all my fault. And rather than take responsibility, apologize, and try to make things right, I did nothing.

I told myself I was being strong, but deep down I knew that what I'd done was cowardly.

I betrayed Marley. And instead of owning up to that fact, I ghosted her.

chapter nine

Next thing I know, I am alone in a gigantic movie theater. No wait, the Girl in Black is here, too, sitting in the front row and holding a bucket of popcorn.

"Want a piece?" she asks, twisting her body around and shaking the popcorn at me. Obviously she's mocking me. And I do not find this funny. Not one bit.

"No," I reply coldly.

"Just one kernel. Come on, Ellie," she teases, a mischievous glint in her blue eyes.

I shake my head in disgust. "I don't know what's going on, but I don't like it. When am I going to wake up from this dream?"

"Oh, so you've settled on a dream state now, have you?" she asks.

"I don't know." I give up and walk down the aisle and sit next to her. The seat is cushy, a little softer than it would be in a regular movie theater. "What's happening now? I'm not exactly in the mood to see a movie."

"Oh, don't you worry. This isn't a movie. It's more like a highlight reel. This is getting old. Dragging you from place to place, year to year, shrinking you down to fit into the snow globe, changing your regular outfit into a bikini for the fish tank, only to go and transform you back to your regular size, etc. . . . I could go on, but why bother? You know where you've been—from one dreary scene to the next. This is much more efficient."

I don't bother arguing with her, and even if I wanted to, I couldn't, because the movie is starting.

The lights in the theater dim. Jumpy jazz music fills the room. The screen lights up and flashes a title card. Bold black letters read:

ELLIE CHARLES, AGES 12–13: THE HIGHLIGHT REEL.
WELCOME TO YOUR LIFE!

Amazingly, twelve-year-old Ellie appears on the screen. As weird as this is, it's also kind of cool. I have always wanted to star in my own reality show—and here it is, already finished. My hair is in a bob and I'm wearing bright pink lipstick. I'm in my favorite store at the mall with my mom. I have just come out of the dressing room wearing the most adorable pair of jeans.

"Wow, these fit me so perfectly and they look amazing. I have to have them!" I tell her, admiring myself in the mirror.

As my mom frowns, worry lines appear between her eyebrows. "I don't know, sweetheart. We got you three new pairs of jeans last week. I don't think you're going to have enough room in your closet for these."

"Then maybe I need a bigger closet," I tell her. My voice is singsongy and I am kind of joking, but also not.

"Oh, Ellie . . ." My mom sounds tired.

I cringe. Maybe this isn't going to be so fun to watch, after all.

"Anyway, it's not only your decision," my younger self reasons up there on the screen. "If you don't get them for me, I can always use my new credit card."

My mom looks tired and slightly annoyed. "Ellie, I know your father gave you a credit card, but that doesn't mean you can buy whatever you want to buy. That doesn't mean you have no limits."

"That's not what he says," I reply. "Dad told me I can have whatever I want. Whenever."

Blech! I totally feel like retching right now. I remember this moment and so many more just like it. At the time, I thought I was being completely reasonable. What's wrong with wanting a cute pair of jeans, after all? But seeing this now? I can't help but think that I'm so incredibly spoiled. Maybe it's the camera angle. I wasn't really this bad. I couldn't have been.

"Who are you trying to convince?" the Girl in Black asks, reading my mind yet again.

"Will you please stop eavesdropping on my private, personal thoughts?" I ask.

Back on the screen, my mom says, "Honey, I think we need to cut back on the shopping."

"And I think I'm calling Dad," Ellie says, whipping her cell phone out of her purse. She dials the number and miraculously, he answers. "Daddy? I'm getting new jeans. That's okay, right? Thanks, Daddy. Actually, can I get two or three pairs? Whatever I want? Thank you."

She looks at her mom, smirking. "Dad says it's fine. You can ask him yourself. Want to talk to him?" She holds the phone up to her mom, knowing that her mom won't take it.

The screen goes black and then there's a new title card that reads:

SIX MONTHS LATER

I'm home and have just answered my front door. Harper is standing there. She's wearing a black ski cap and her hair is tucked up into it. "You'll never guess what I did," she tells me, exuberant. I've never seen her so happy, and this annoys me for some reason.

"What?" I ask sharply, crossing my arms across my chest.

When Harper pulls off her hat, her long silky hair tumbles down. She's a natural brunette, but now, suddenly she has blond streaks. "Don't you love it?" she asks, so excited As she shakes her head, her hair literally cascades down her back. It's so pretty I want to scream. "I couldn't wait to show you. I knew you'd flip! I still can't believe my parents let me do it. I've been begging for ages and I used every last cent of my babysitting money to pay for it. That was the deal."

My eyes seriously bug out. I cannot believe this. Harper looks absolutely stunning—too much so. It's not simply her hair, it's the way her entire face lights up. She is radiant and glowing, and it's killing me.

I don't say anything right away. I remember contemplating, wondering, *How am I going to play this? This isn't going to work. No friend of mine can outdo me. I need to be the brightest star in the room.*

Then I see the smile on my face—that metaphorical light-bulb-flashing-in-my-brain moment. I have a brilliant idea.

"Of course I love it, Harper. But I cannot believe you copied me. What kind of friend are you? Incapable of an original thought?" I ask.

"Huh?" Harper replies, her features clouding over into confusion.

"You know I'm getting blond highlights tomorrow," I tell her.

"What? I didn't know," Harper says, as her expression shifts from slightly nervous to genuine panic. "That's crazy. I swear, Ellie. Honestly, I had no idea. Wow, what a funny coincidence. Great minds think alike, huh?"

She keeps running her hands through her hair, as if trying to protect or claim what is rightfully hers, but it's not going to work.

This isn't about who is right or wrong. This is about me getting what I want.

"Come on, Harper. I value honesty in our friendship

above all else. It hurts my feelings when you lie to my face."

She bites her bottom lip, which is trembling. She looks down. "I swear I didn't know. I'm not lying—please believe me."

"Oh, I see. So you're saying *I'm* a liar?" I ask.

"Gosh, no. I guess maybe you told me and, and, and I wasn't paying attention?" She's so nervous she's practically stuttering.

Now I've got Harper exactly where I want her. This is almost too easy. I suppress my smile.

"It's okay, Harper. I know you don't have the best memory."

Harper stares at me, unsure. Clearly she is not buying this. But she also has no interest in standing up to me. She is weak, putty in my hands! I love that this is going to be so easy. And I justify it by telling myself it'll teach her a good lesson. Train her to stand up for herself. Not now with me, of course. I mean next time. With other people.

"So I guess now we'll match," she tries, giving me a pathetic half smile, like she knows she's not getting off this easily.

I laugh in her face. "Nice try, babe. You know that we're too old to have matching hairstyles, right?"

Harper nods, for the moment relieved. "Yes, absolutely. I totally agree with you there."

"Good, then it's settled," I say. "I'm so glad you can be reasonable about this."

"Phew." She sighs, thinking she's off the hook. "Hey, did you ever think about dying your hair red?" she asks. "Because that would be super cute."

I smile at her, and shake my head ever so slowly. "Oh, Harper. That's not the answer. My mom already made the appointment, and it's with the top colorist in town—Hector at Cush Salon. She had to pull a lot of strings to get him to fit me in. His waiting list is six months long. So I can't back out. It's way too late."

I am making this up as I go along, which is a little nerve-wracking, until I realize that Harper has no idea. She believes me completely. Turns out I am an excellent liar. "Anyway, to make a long story short," I continue, "you need to get rid of yours."

"Wait, what do you mean get rid of mine?" asks Harper.

Ellie doesn't say anything at first. Simply smiles at her.

Harper coughs and squirms. "I guess they'll grow out in time," she adds.

"Oh, that's not going to work. You know I can't wait

that long. Hold on. Let me help you out," I tell her. I run to my room and come back a moment later with a pair of scissors. "Why don't we go to the bathroom so you can do this in the mirror," I suggest, holding them out to her.

She eyes the scissors warily, not budging. She looks over her shoulder, probably contemplating whether or not she can get away with making a run for it.

I can't let that happen. "Come on, it's only hair, Harper. I'll help. Follow me."

I head to the bathroom and she trails me.

Let me point out that she follows me—I in no way physically coerce her to go along with the plan. I'm proud of this.

I stop once we get there, and we both stare at her image in the mirror. "Do you want to do it or should I?" I ask.

And before she can stop me, I grab a giant hunk of hair on the side of her head and snip. Fast—just like that it's gone.

Her eyes go wide and her face turns pale. "Wait!" she yells.

"Oh, of course. You probably want to do the honors. Silly me," I say, handing her the scissors.

She opens her mouth as if to protest but doesn't say a word. We stare at each other for a few moments. Her expression switches from shock to annoyance to sadness to resignation. She knows better than to challenge me. It's a harsh reality, yet the reality nonetheless. There is no way out for her. No happy ending to this tale.

Finally she nods. "Good idea."

And I watch her cut off her hair. She does it slowly at first. Her hand trembles and her eyes are moist, but she's determined not to cry. It's shaggy and uneven and absolutely atrocious. I'm frankly shocked she's managing to hold herself together.

Once she's finally finished, I clap my hands together and exclaim, "That's adorable!"

The entire screen freezes on a close-up of my face. I was so absorbed in the moment I almost forgot I was watching this unfold on the screen.

I sink down further into my seat. "What is the point of this?" I ask.

"Wait, there's more," the Girl in Black replies.

She snaps her fingers and the scene changes again. Now we're back at school, near my locker. I'm thirteen and in conversation with Serena, a new girl who just moved to Lincoln Heights from Houston. She's got dark braids and big brown eyes and glasses and, of course, she wants to be my new BFF. And of course, that is not going to happen. Not that she knows it yet.

162

Serena hands me a book report. I flip through the pages. "This is your best work, yes?"

"Of course." Serena nods. "I did yours first and spent the most time on it. I hardly had time to finish my own work."

I level my gaze at her, sizing her up, wondering why she's telling me this, what she wants from me. Sympathy? Not gonna happen!

I shrug. "Not my problem. Maybe you should manage your time better."

"Yes, Ellie. Of course. You are right. You are always right." Now Serena sounds too eager to please.

I look through the report, scanning it quickly, and then toss it in the garbage.

"What are you doing?" she asks, gasping.

"Oh, I did my own homework," I tell her. "I don't need yours."

"Then, then why did you ask me to do it for you?"

"It was a test," I say carefully, narrowing my eyes.

She relaxes. "Oh, so I passed. I'm a good enough friend to cheat for you? Is this like some crazy loyalty thing? I'm so relieved you're not going to actually use it because that did seem a little weird."

Serena thinks she's gotten me figured out, that things are that simple. This annoys me even more. Because yes, she called it exactly—that was my original plan. But now I've got to come up with something better. Change tactics. Be unpredictable.

That's one secret to maintaining my power. No one can know what to expect. If I change the rules all the time, I keep everyone on their toes.

I shake my head slowly. "It was a test, but not one of friendship," I say. "By cheating, you revealed your true moral character. Now I know I can't trust you. If you were a real friend, and a stand-up kind of person, you would have refused to do my book report for me because it's wrong and risky, plus you'd be robbing me of an educational opportunity. Don't you know I'm the top student at this school? I don't need to cheat."

"Oh," she says, staring at the paper in the garbage can. Just then Molly Bowie walks by and tosses a crumpled chocolate milk container on top of it. Some of the milk drips onto it and Serena cringes. I grin, because I couldn't have orchestrated this moment better if I'd tried.

"You should have stood up to me, refused to do my work and risk putting me in harm's way. That's how a true friend would act. That's what Harper and Maddie and Lily would've done." (I am making this part up. Everyone knows that Harper, Maddie, and Lily do whatever I tell them to do without thinking. That is why we are all such good friends.)

Serena doesn't seem to know what to do. She stares at me, uncomprehending.

I gaze right back at her, steadily, waiting.

"Well, then. Okay," she finally says. "I failed. So now what?" She gulps, staring at me with tears in her eyes.

It's a great question.

I actually don't have an answer. I didn't expect things to turn out this way. I didn't really think Serena would write the paper for me. It's especially insulting because everyone knows I'm the smartest kid in school. And yes, she's only been here for a few weeks, but it's one of the first things she should've learned.

"So, what do you think should happen now?" I ask, crossing my arms over my chest.

"Oh, I think I should apologize, which I'm going to do right now, regardless. I'm sorry, Ellie. I'm sorry I insulted your intelligence. I didn't mean to. But mostly, I'm sorry I failed the test, sorry I let you down. Sorry I may not get to hang out with you and your friends. Because you all seem so awesome. Your whole group does."

Hmmm. This is nice to hear. "Go on," I say.

"Oh, I was done," she says.

"No, I want to hear more. About how awesome we are."

"Well, you and Harper and Lily and Maddie and, well, mostly you. Everyone knows you are the most popular kids in school. You have so much fun. And I mean, each one of you is better-looking than the next."

I raise one eyebrow at this news.

She notices, and gasps, brings her hand to her lips like she made a mistake.

"I mean, excluding you. No one can compare to you. You're, like, on a whole different level, and I just want to hang out with you guys. Please?"

No one has ever begged me to be their friend before. It's kind of an ego trip, but also crazy enough to arouse suspicion. Who is this weirdo? Her desperation is bringing me down.

"I'll think about it," I say. "Let's talk next week."

With that, I turn on my heel and head out.

My plan is to keep her hanging, and that is exactly what I do. At first I think I'll ignore her for a few days—a week, tops. But instead, I never get back to her.

And it was a good trick. I pulled the same thing with Daisy Harris, who moved to town from South Dakota a week later. Wasn't as much fun the second time around. When she broke down in real tears, I thought I'd feel empowered, but instead it was just embarrassing. For everyone.

So I tried it a third time with this girl named Zara, who transferred from Catholic school. Not only did I make her do my history homework, I told her she had to wear the plaid skirt from her uniform for two weeks in a row. It's amazing what people will do.

Of course, after Zara people began to expect this type of hazing, so I had to switch things up. Sofia had always been around in the background, but we'd never hung out. I decided to adopt her as my new best friend. It was a good move, expanding the group. It made us all more powerful and it kept my other friends on their toes. Let them know they weren't that special, that they could always be replaced.

Anyway, the meaner, more demanding, more difficult that I am, the more kids fear me, and the more kids fear me, the more they want to hang out with me.

It's fun. Invigorating. I have tried on this identity and it fits me perfectly, like that gorgeous leather jacket Ruby Silano got for her birthday and then regifted to me the very next day. Just because. No special occasion . . . other than the fact that I made her do it, I mean.

Sure, sometimes I think about the way I walk all over people and I cringe over the callousness.

But the more I do it, the more I get used to it.

It's fun.

It's who I am.

Or it's who I have become, anyway.

It certainly beats the alternative.

When the lights go on I turn to the Girl in Black. "Okay, I get it. I'm a horrible, rotten person. What else is new?"

"You tell me," she replies.

I am so sick of this trip down memory lane. Plus, I haven't even brought up the fact that this is so selective. "You are only showing me the bad. The rotten scenes. Everything I've done wrong. You haven't mentioned any of the positive stuff."

"Like what?" the Girl in Black asks.

"Like, how I'm a role model for my fellow students. How I have raised the bar so high here at Lincoln Heights Middle School, it forces everyone to work even harder. How everyone aspires to be as perfect as me."

Rather than answer me with words, she lets out a big laugh.

And that's when I realize that nothing is keeping me here inside this movie theater. There are no beaded curtain bars. I'm not trapped in some cheap plexiglass snow globe, or an actual-glass fish tank. Plus, the film is over. The lights are even on. So I stand up and head for the exit. I'm thinking I'll be free from the Girl in Black, and back in the gym and in my regular thirteen-year-old body, as originally planned, but instead my feet get swept up from under me and suddenly I'm on my back. Everything happens so quickly, it takes a few moments to realize what's what: I'm in a sled whooshing down a snowy mountain. I zip past pine trees and snowmen and woodland creatures. This scene is familiar, but I have never been sledding here before. Honestly, it's gorgeous, magical. When I zoom past a few red birds I realize where I am—in the mural!

This is crazy. Every other place I've been to since this nightmare began actually exists in real life. But this scene? Jack and Dezi and Reese and those other theater geeks—they made this. Someone imagined this snowy scene and came up with a design and executed it. Yet it feels so real.

It makes me wonder . . . I mean, sure I'm good at taking tests and reading social situations and jockeying for power, getting what I want, manipulating people. Those sorts of things. But what have I ever actually made? Except for misery and fear?

Of course, I have my reasons. Making other people feel bad and weak distracts me from my own pain. And it props me up. But is that good enough?

I think about the conscious choice I made so many years ago. When faced with those mean girls, I was weak, afraid, shy. And I promised myself I would change. I vowed to turn myself into one of them for protection. Because that pain I felt? It overwhelmed me. I didn't want to hurt that badly ever again. But I wonder if there was another choice. If I could've gone in another direction.

Marley did. She was different. She chose to be kind. While I chose the opposite.

I thought I was making myself strong by being cold and calculating and steely. But at what cost?

As I have this thought I see something alarming up ahead: a cliff. I'm racing toward it. I look for the brakes, but there are no brakes. Well, of course not. I'm on a sled!

What if I speed off the cliff? Will this nightmare end? Maybe it's about time I find out. It's not like I have a choice in the matter. Better to simply let it happen.

I hold my breath and squeeze my eyes shut tight and I feel the lift and suddenly I'm sailing. I'm flying through the air.

It's exhilarating. I finally feel free.

At least until I crash-land.

chapter ten

I'm in the gym. I've come right through the mural, which still exists, has not yet been destroyed by me. In fact it now has track marks in the snow, charting the path I took on the sled. That's kind of cool—I've made my mark on the thing. It's proof that I'm not crazy and hallucinating. Or maybe it's proof that my hallucinations are incredibly detailed . . . Time will tell. Or not. Either way, it's a relief to be back in familiar territory, back to the present.

And it's funny, I expected to find myself on the ground, but I'm still standing. And wait a second . . . I hear someone yelling. And that someone sounds distinctly like me. I walk toward the crowd that has gathered at the far end of the gym and that's when I see myself ranting. I am still two people, it seems. The "me" me is still invisible.

And then there's visible me, who is screaming at the top of her lungs. "No one thinks winter wonderland and birds. The two concepts don't even belong in the same sentence!"

Oh right. This is around an hour before the fall. Visible me is wrapping things up. That means that invisible me can watch myself scream at Reese for putting those stupid birds in the mural.

Birds that, I now have to admit, are really cool-looking.

The theater geeks stand behind Reese, stunned. Jack stares at me, openmouthed.

The entire gym is watching.

This is real power.

This is control.

At least I think it is.

I know the Girl in Black keeps taking me to scenes from my past that make me look bad, but obviously there are reasons for my behavior, explanations that made perfect sense at the time. I needed to assert myself, transform from the meek little girl I used to be into someone strong. And I have.

These kids fear me.

They try to defend themselves but they can't.

I watch as visible me holds on to the mural, and Reese tries to pull it away. Visible me is not letting go. It tears and she cringes. Oh, how she cringes.

Visible me's face screws up into a look of annoyance. It flashes to anger and then rage as she tears the whole thing in half.

The crowd gasps. Emboldened by their horror, visible me grabs the mural and tears it up again and again and again, until it's useless confetti, which she throws in Reese's face. "Oops!" she says. "Well, at least we have more snow."

Aside from Sofia's forced laugh, the entire gym is silent.

Three kids from the theater department are crying now. I didn't notice this the first time around.

Ugh. Something in my heart hurts.

I have this new crazy thought: Seeing myself from the outside? I don't seem so powerful, so in control. I kind of seem like a monster. But I am not. I know I am not. Even if I sometimes behave like one . . .

I have my reasons.

Suddenly a phone rings.

"Who left their cell phone on during my meeting?" visible me yells. Then a second later, when no one cops to it she goes, "Hah, that's me. Get to work, everyone. String those lights. Hang the murals. Put out the snow. Find something cool for the fourth wall . . ."

Visible me answers the call and leaves through the double doors of the auditorium. Where she talks to her dad, does her nails, and power walks. Been there. Done that. Yawn! This time I am sticking around.

I want to watch this magic happen, see my committee work smoothly without me, their leader.

For the first time since this nightmare began, I'm actually digging this whole invisibility thing and looking forward to watching the scene unfold. I've always wanted to witness my classmates gush about how much they love and appreciate me, and marvel over the vast number of sacrifices I have made for this school. How I am so awesome at everything, it inspires them to achieve their very best. I remember ducking back into the gym after my power walk and seeing it transformed, like magic. Now I'll be able to witness that process. See this smoothly run operation that I put into motion, a well-oiled machine. I can't wait.

First I walk over to the theater geeks. They are

consoling Reese, who is actually crying. Well, okay. It makes sense that she's upset. I came on a little, well, intense. But I know she'll come around. Winter birds— how dumb! She's lucky I pointed it out before the entire school showed up to witness such foolishness.

"All that hard work. And the fourth mural was the best one of the bunch. What kind of monster does something like that?" she asks.

Jack rubs her back. "Don't worry about it. We still have three and a half murals to hang up. And the work is stunning. Each scene is so detailed, so gorgeous. You are so talented, Reese. I'll bet Ellie is jealous."

Wait, what? Is he serious? "I'm not jealous of you theater geeks. What a joke!" I yell.

"Haven't you figured it out yet—no one can hear you," the Girl in Black replies snarkily. I hadn't even noticed her in the room, lurking around in silent judgment, as usual.

"I know that. I'm just venting!" I shout back.

"He's totally right, Reese. She's an evil, jealous, pathetic monster, and I cannot wait to graduate and be free of her," says Charlie.

"Oh, it'll be the same in high school. Don't you think?" asks Jack.

Reese sniffs and wipes her nose with the back of her hand. "Maybe worse," she says.

"There is no way she can be worse," Dezi points out.

Hmmm . . . This is unexpected. Yes, I did tear up their work. The wounds are still fresh, but I know that eventually they will come to understand that I did them a huge favor. And if not, then who cares what these theater geeks think? They have too many pimples to matter.

I move on to my real friends, to Harper and Sofia and Maddie and Lily, who are hanging the string lights.

"Is this straight?" asks Sofia, holding up a strand.

"It looks straight enough to me, but I can't say for sure because I'm not Ellie Charles," Harper grumbles.

"Luckily," Maddie says with a laugh.

Lily sighs and asks, "Why does she have to be so bossy?"

"Don't stress. It's almost vacation. Soon we'll get a break," Maddie replies.

"Not soon enough," says Harper. "She's worse than ever."

"I think I officially hate her," says Sofia.

"Don't say that. She'll hear you," warns Harper.

"But she's not even here," Sofia points out. "She's off

on the phone, probably renegotiating her deal with the devil."

The rest of the girls giggle at this. Deal with the devil? That's crazy, and I can't believe they're talking about me behind my back like this.

I'm not that bad.

I don't think so, anyway.

"Guys, be careful. You know she must have spies," says Maddie, looking around with suspicion. "Or maybe she bugged the entire gym."

Harper shudders nervously. "I'm so freaked out right now. You're probably right."

"I was kidding," says Maddie. "I mean—kidding, not kidding!"

Everyone laughs.

"I wouldn't put it past her, though," says Harper.

"I know," says Maddie. And everyone else agrees with her.

"Wait a second. Are you people serious? This is how you treat me when I'm not around to defend myself? You'd be nothing without me," I shout.

The Girl in Black pops up next to me suddenly.

"I know they can't hear me!" I scream impatiently. "So don't even bother saying it."

"Okay," she replies, folding her arms over her chest. "But you could've fooled me."

I groan. This is too much to take. Stupid middle school dance committee. Amateurs and babies, every single one of them. I have had enough! I turn on my heel and head for the exit. Except when I walk through the double doors, I end up in . . .

Wait a moment . . .

Where am I?

Could this be?

Yes, I am finally in Hawaii!

chapter eleven

This is more like it. I am standing in the middle of a huge hotel room. It's bright and spotless. On one wall there's a blond wood dresser with a gorgeous pink orchid in the middle of it. Against the other wall is the softest-looking bed I have ever seen, with a gazillion fluffy white pillows on top. Below me is a cream-colored rug.

I am wearing a cute purple minidress and one of those Hawaiian-flowered-necklace things—a lei. And it's adorable. I am adorable. There's a gigantic full-size mirror here, as well, so I have proof.

Over the dresser is a beautiful photo of the ocean. And to the left of that—something even better: the actual ocean. It's so blue and sparkly!

I go out onto the balcony to get a closer look, to take in the scent of it. Yes, I have a balcony. How awesome is this? It's hard to see how things can get any better.

And no, the recent past does not make any sense, but if I had to go through that crazy, horrible ordeal to end up here, well then so be it. I am in Hawaii and ready to have the best vacation of my life.

I lean forward and gaze at the gorgeous view and take in a deep breath so I can smell the fresh, salty air.

Then I hear someone behind me. "What are you still doing in my room?" a strange woman asks.

I spin around, confused. She seems to be speaking directly to me, but how is that possible? I've been invisible for so long, I thought I'd never reappear as an actual, living, breathing human. But here I am, no longer a ghost.

I am back in my own body, and in a cute sundress. So cool! But how did this happen? I seemed to have skipped a few steps in between falling off the ladder and ending up on this island.

Did I somehow sleepwalk through the entire dance? And still manage to pack, sneak out of the house, get to the airport and on a plane, and then arrive here? To this gorgeous hotel room?

Or is there magic still happening? Did the Girl in Black lead me through some sort of metaphysical time warp? Or maybe I'm overthinking things. I don't know how to figure this out, so maybe I should just enjoy it.

After all, I'm in Hawaii!

"Hi," I say, waving to the tall woman who has stepped outside to join me. At first I figure she must be the housekeeper, but on second glance I think not. She's dressed too fancy to clean a room. She's tall and blond and tan and in a white, silky, sleeveless jumpsuit. She's got on white, platform-heeled sandals, which must add five inches to her already considerable height. This woman is an Amazon and dripping in diamonds—from her ears, to her neck, to her fingers.

"I said, what are you doing in my room?" she asks, and not very kindly.

"Oh, I think you must be mistaken. I'm Ellie Charles and this is my room. And my balcony. I think. I mean, I assume this is where I'm supposed to be. I'm meeting my dad here. His name is Nick and—"

She holds up her hand and says, "Yes, I know all that. I only wish your father had prepared you better, instead of leaving everything up to me."

"Wait, you know my dad?" I ask.

"Of course I do. I'm Nikka, his fiancée."

I blink a few times, stare at this woman. "I'm sorry . . . his what?" I ask.

"Didn't you read the note?" she asks.

"Note?" I am completely confused, with no idea what this woman is talking about. My dad can't have a fiancée. That would be too crazy. How could he not tell me? And where is he, anyway? "I think you must be in the wrong room," I tell her. "There's got to be some kind of mistake . . ."

She shakes her head. "No, you're the one in the wrong room," she says.

She walks over to my bedside table, picks up a small envelope, and shows me the front of it:

To Ellie, it reads.

"Um, I kind of just arrived. I guess I didn't have time to open it?"

She smirks, unimpressed, and opens the letter for me.

"Hey, wait. That's addressed to me!"

She holds out her hand. "Yeah, and you already failed to read it so I'm going to do it for you. Ready? Listen up, because I don't want to do this twice." She clears her throat and begins.

" 'Dear Ellie,

Great news. I'm engaged to Nikka Prune. She is a model I met while working in Romania last month. I know you two will have a lot in common and I wish I could introduce you in person, but there was an emergency in Denmark that I had to attend to. Merry Christmas! Please enjoy yourself. Think of it as a great opportunity to bond with Nikka. I know you two will have fun. I will try to make it back in a few days, and if not, well, I'm sad to have missed you.

"Love, Daddy.'"

"Is this a joke?" I ask, moving toward Nikka and the note.

"'P.S.,'" she reads. "'Your room is downstairs on the other side of the resort, next to the maid's quarters. You are too young to have a room this spectacular. If your vacation is this cushy now, what will you have to look forward to?'"

"It does not say that," I reply.

"Read it for yourself," Nikka says, handing it over.

I scan the note quickly. The words are all there, except the postscript looks like it was added more recently. The handwriting doesn't match and the ink is even a different color.

"My dad didn't write the part about me having to give up my room," I say. I squint more closely at the letter. "And what's this bit that's crossed out? Something about me being allowed to charge whatever I want to his account? I need to talk to my dad immediately."

"Well, your dad isn't here now, is he?" Nikka asks, raising her thinly plucked eyebrows. "So maybe you should stop complaining and start packing."

My heart sinks. Tears well up in my eyes. I blink furiously to hold them back. I don't even care about the room, necessarily. It's the news, which is so typical. This note. My dad. I should've known. No matter how perfect I am, how cool and in control, I always fall for it. Again and again.

It doesn't matter that I'm on the honor roll, at the top of my class, a straight-A student, popular, and well-dressed, the leader of every school committee that matters. My dad doesn't care. He doesn't even seem to know me. And he doesn't bother trying, either. We make plans to see each other. I get my hopes up. I think we're going to spend time together. And then he flakes.

"This can't be happening. Where are you, Girl in Black?" I shout, looking around the room, under the bed, behind the mirror, in the bathroom and closet.

Nikka stares at me. "Your father didn't tell me you were crazy."

"Wait, what? You can't say that. I'm not crazy!" I insist, spinning around to face her.

She shrugs. "Oh well. I suppose it doesn't really matter."

"Is your last name actually Prune?" I ask.

"For now," says Nikka. "But soon it will be Charles."

"Right." I think about this for a few moments. "So that means you'll be my . . . stepmother?"

"Oh, technically, but please don't call me that. Ever. I mean, come on, Ellie. I'm way too young to be a mother of any kind. Even step."

It's true. She barely looks old enough to be my baby-sitter. Not that I need a babysitter anymore. "Well, what should I call you?" I wonder.

"Everyone calls me Nikka. You can do the same. Or call me whatever you want. I really don't care. Your dad promised me you wouldn't be around that much."

I didn't think things could get any worse, and then they did. "He actually said that?" I shake my head. "No, it's impossible. I don't believe you."

This is what I tell her, but deep down I have my doubts. Maybe I am a nuisance. Maybe I'm the reason my dad left us in the first place. Maybe he never even wanted a child.

That thought sits there, an icy cold feeling in my chest.

I'm close to tears and it's obvious, but Nikka couldn't care less. She smiles coldly and picks up her purse.

"Well, I'm late for a spa appointment. See you later."
She waves and heads for the door.

"Wait!" I call.

"Yes?" she asks.

"Um, can I come to the spa with you?"

She laughs and crosses her arms over her chest and glares at me like I'm a cockroach she found in her soup. "Oh, Ellie. *I'm* going to the spa. *We're* not going to the spa. You, my dear, are busy. You've got to change rooms. And after that, well, I'm not going to sit around and entertain you all day. You're a big girl. You can get lunch at the pool, but don't order anything too expensive, okay?"

"Um . . ."

Before I can say another word, she is gone.

I whip out my phone and call my dad. He doesn't pick up. I send him a text. *CALL ME!!!!*

I wait, but he doesn't respond. There are no three dots that he is typing, even. He must be on the phone. I sit in my room and wait.

And wait.

And wait.

I can't believe my dad flew me to Hawaii only to go to Denmark without me, before I even arrived.

I can't believe he got engaged and didn't tell me.

And I can't believe Nikka. What is her problem?

How am I supposed to spend Christmas with someone I've never met before? Someone who so clearly
doesn't want to have anything to do with me? It's absurd.
And I miss my mom. It's hard to admit it, but I do. I made
a mistake. Messed up big-time. What was I thinking?
How could I be so awful? Ugh. I flop down on the bed,
faceup, and stare at the ceiling. This stinks.

But wait a second, despite this ridiculous situation,
I'm still in Hawaii. What am I complaining about? So
Nikka doesn't want to go to the spa with me. So she seems
to be angry with me, even though we've never met. She
wouldn't act this way if my dad were around, I don't
think. And maybe we won't have to spend time together
alone again. I can make sure of that.

I try my dad again and the phone goes right to
voicemail.

Is he ignoring my calls?

No, he is probably in an important meeting. I'm sure
he'll call me as soon as he has a moment. I text him,
Emergency, so he knows how important this is.

Then I try to relax. I need to make the most of this
vacation. Especially since I totally bragged to every single one of my friends, and plenty of my enemies, and the
lady who sold me this sundress, about going to Hawaii.
What am I going to tell them now? That I cried in my

hotel room the whole time? There's no way. I must save face. Turn things around. This trip is a disaster, but no one else has to know how miserable the situation is. The sun still shines. The ocean is still blue. I am still gorgeous. And my wardrobe is fabulous.

I drag myself out of bed and splash cold water onto my face. Figuring I can change rooms later (or never, if I actually get to speak with my dad), I put on my favorite pink bikini, the matching sarong, and flip-flops, and head to the pool.

Grabbing a soft white towel, I place it on an empty lounge chair with a view of the pool and beach. This is more like it. On the surface, I am in paradise.

And surface stuff matters. So do pictures. I must remember who I am, where I come from. Everything that matters to me. There's so much pressure to maintain my picture-perfect image. Otherwise I won't be envied. And what's the opposite of envy? Pity. I will not go back there.

So I pull my phone from my purse, and position myself so I'm in the shot with the ocean and pool in the background.

I smile like mad and click. Then I take a few more shots in different positions. I change my lipstick and do some close-ups with duck lips. I take a picture of my hand holding a glass of strawberry lemonade, zooming in on the fresh mint leaf floating on top. And then I sit back and scroll through my options. So many amazing shots to choose from! I post one, then sit back and relax.

Then I close my eyes.

Except it's too loud to actually nap. There are so many kids at this resort, laughing and having fun. I prop myself up on my elbows and watch.

In the pool are three kids, siblings, I assume, swimming around one tall dude—obviously the dad. They are rowdy and rambunctious, pushing and shoving and yelling and laughing. The littlest one is a girl who is around eight. She is holding on to a donut-shaped floatie. It's got pink frosting with rainbow sprinkles on top. And her tank suit matches it perfectly. Like they came as a set.

The other two are boys—maybe twins, or maybe they are simply really close in age. One is blond and one has red hair and they both have matching blue-and-yellow-striped swim trunks. All three hang on their dad, who throws them across the pool, one by one. They scream with delight.

"More, more, more!"

"Higher!"

"Faster!"

"Me next!"

Soon a woman approaches, and the little girl's eyes light up. "Mommy, Mommy, come in!" she screams.

"I will in a bit," the mom says, kneeling down and feeling the water. "I need to take care of some things first, though. What does everyone want to do for dinner? We can go to that pizza place from the other night, or try sushi this time."

"Pizza!" the kids all yell.

"And then I need to sign up for the mountain biking tour. Should we do that later this afternoon or tomorrow morning?"

"Tomorrow!" They are chipper and cheerful and in agreement. They remind me of baby birds, for some reason.

"Okay, then. Let me make those reservations and change into my suit and then I'll join you."

"Yay!" the boys cheer. The dad grabs the kid closest to him and throws him again. *Splash!*

I watch as the mom laughs and shakes her head at the silliness. She's joyful as she walks away. She won at life. Clearly.

I wonder what that's like—being part of a big, happy family?

I try to imagine the life I could've had if my parents

had stayed together. Or the vacation that my mom and I might have gone on with Marley and her dads, the many vacations by now, if only I hadn't betrayed her. If I hadn't ghosted her.

Instead I have Mom, and it's always so quiet at my house. I wonder what she's going to do for Christmas.

She'll be all alone. We never have plans these days. I wonder if she even realizes I'm gone. I didn't leave a note, I don't think. I didn't have the opportunity to write one, but that's just a pathetic excuse—I never planned on leaving her a note. I meant to text her from Hawaii, and scrolling through my old messages, I can see I haven't yet done so.

I should text her now. But what am I supposed to say?

I am rotten. Worse. I am treating my mom in the same way that my dad treats me. Why am I doing that? I hate how my dad treats me.

What have I done?

Ugh! I don't want to think about this so I put my phone away again. Why am I so worried? There is nothing I can do. I am in Hawaii. I should do something fun. Make the most of my time here. Do something beach-y. Like, I know. I'll go for a swim.

I stand up and stretch and walk to the edge of the deep end. Then I dive into the pool.

The water is cool and refreshing. I swim a lap or two

and then decide to do a somersault. Except, when I emerge from the water, I'm in a bathtub.

Weird . . .

I look around, and see that I am not simply in any bathtub. I'm in my own bathtub—the one back in Lincoln Heights.

It's kind of creepy, but maybe good, as well, because I was feeling a little guilty about going to Hawaii without telling my mom. Maybe I'm still real, and simply magic. It sure seems that way. In the bathtub, I see I'm in the same pink bikini.

But as soon as I pull myself out, I find myself fully clothed and dry as a bone.

"Cool effect," I call out to the Girl in Black.

She ignores me and I find this irritating.

"That was a compliment," I tell her.

No response. Oh well.

I wander into the living room and find my mom.

"Hi there!" I say, but she doesn't even look up. "Hello?" I wave my hand in front of her face. It seems that I'm invisible again. I hang back and observe.

My mom is staring at her computer screen. The overhead lamp is switched off, but the pale-blue glow from the screen lights up her face.

And I see pain in her eyes, tears running down her cheeks.

I wonder what she's looking at. I walk around the couch and lean over her shoulder so I can see the screen.

Oh wow. She's pulled up my Instagram account. My mom is looking at pictures of me, in Hawaii, posing with the beach in the background and a huge fake smile plastered onto my face. I look so happy and glamorous on the surface. Anyone who saw this shot would think my life was perfect, that I was the luckiest kid around and exactly where I wanted to be. My mom certainly seems to have this impression.

She's looking at me and her fingertips brush the computer screen and she's crying. Because she thinks I'm having an amazing time without her.

And suddenly I realize something even worse—I didn't even get my mom a present, didn't even send her a postcard or call her on Christmas.

My heart aches for her and my entire insides feel rotten.

I know I won't be able to touch her but I need to try. I reach out and place my hand on my mom's shoulder.

And then another crazy thing happens.

Within a millisecond I am gone—again.

chapter twelve

Now I am somewhere else—in yet another new gym. This one smells freshly painted. It's got shiny, polished wood floors. In the middle of the basketball court is the image of a roaring lion with the words LINCOLN HEIGHTS LIONS written around it. The logo is painted orange and black and white. I've seen the insignia before—the lion is our town's high school mascot. So this must be the high school gym. Things are beginning to come together. And suddenly it dawns on me. I look around for the Girl in Black. I don't see her but sense she is nearby.

"I get it now. You are taking me on a journey of my past, present, and future. How awesome! I've totally seen this movie!"

"Have you?" The Girl in Black ducks out from behind red velvet curtains onstage. She hops down to my level and walks on over.

"Yes," I say, proud of myself. "I figured it out."

"You know it was a book before it was a movie?" she asks.

"Whatever," I say.

"Hah. And you're supposed to be so smart."

"What's your point?" I ask.

"Maybe you should stop acting like a mean girl from some dumb movie and start acting like a real human being with emotions and empathy and a heart and a conscience."

I cross my arms over my chest and give her my best withering glare. "I thought you said it was a book first."

"It was, but I'm trying to dumb this down so you can understand it," the Girl in Black says with a shrug. Before I can remind her that I am a straight-A student, the double doors open up and future me strides on in.

Wow! I am amazed, truly awestruck. Future me is even more fabulous than I imagined possible. She's wearing five-inch heels and the most beautiful prom dress I have ever seen in my whole entire life. It's white and silver and strapless, equal parts clingy and free-flowing. It's got crystal beads sewn into the bodice, reminiscent of the pink Clara costume I never got to wear onstage for *The Nutcracker*. When she walks, she seems to glide on air, like a princess from another galaxy.

Then things get even better. A cute boy walks in next. He's got dark hair and blue eyes and he's dressed in a really nice black tuxedo with a silver cummerbund that matches future me's gown. He must be my date.

"The gym looks amazing, Ellie. People are going to flip," he says.

He's right. And I must be in charge because I love the whole look of the room. It's totally my style: French-garden themed, with beds of lavender and trellises covered in sweet-smelling wisteria. White gauzy tablecloths cover the tables. And there are ornate silver platters— empty for now, but I'm sure whatever food I ordered is going to be delicious.

Future me walks right up to him and wraps her arms around his neck and says, "I sure hope so, considering how hard it was, managing everyone and pulling this thing together."

"You do make it look so easy, though," he replies.

"And you look scrumptious, boyfriend," she says, tilting her head up, ever so gently, so she can gaze into his big, beautiful eyes.

"Thanks," he replies.

"And me?" she asks.

He looks her up and down, grinning. "There are no words," he says.

Meanwhile, I swoon. We are a picture-perfect couple. I reach for my phone so I can take a picture, but of course I don't have it on me. I guess I only get my phone when I'm not invisible, like in Hawaii. Interesting. I'm getting used to this universe, this state of being, this, whatever one would call it. I now know to expect the unexpected. And future me is such an awesome surprise. I can now sit back and bask in the glory of it all, my future, my success.

"I told you everything would work out," I say to the Girl in Black. "Sometimes you have to be ruthless, to harden your heart to go after what you want, what's really important."

"Just wait," the Girl in Black tells me. "This isn't over yet."

I laugh in her face. "Oh, you're only bluffing. You probably don't even know what's happening next. Looks to me like I had a goal and worked really hard and succeeded. Sure I had to step on some toes to get there, hurt some feelings, but so what? I get exactly what I want out of life, so why are you trying to bring down my mood? I don't need that."

"Do you actually think your life is so perfect?" she asks.

"Okay, so Hawaii was a little rough. That's okay. And maybe my friends do talk about me behind my back, but isn't that normal?"

"Is it? Would all your friends do that?"

I think of Marley, of how true and sincere she was. How honest and pure her heart is. How even after I betrayed her, she would've forgiven me.

The Girl in Black and I lock eyes. Something about her seems so familiar. It gives me the chills.

I'm about to ask her who she is, when she gives me this strange little smile and then disappears. Well, who needs her? Not me. I turn around and watch future me laugh with her boyfriend.

She throws back her head and shakes out her hair and grins. "You are too sweet, my love," she says to him.

He smiles down at her and gently cups her face in his hands and then kisses her on the tip of her nose.

Wait, what?

A nose kiss?

Suddenly the romance of this entire scene comes to a screeching halt. What kind of high school boyfriend kisses you on the nose? Not the kind I thought I would have.

I am confused, and so is my future self. I can tell by the way her shoulders tense up and her head tilts to the side, ever so slightly.

Future me looks at her boyfriend with narrowed eyes. "What's up, Jeremy?"

Wait a second. Did she just say Jeremy? I take a step closer and blink a few times. Looking at the guy more carefully, I realize I know him. This is insane!

Future me is going out with Jeremy Hinkey. As in Jeremy Fartburger. The same Jeremy I kicked out of my Winter Holiday Semiformal planning committee meeting in the eighth grade is now my prom date when I'm a senior? And it seems that he's my boyfriend, too?

More surprisingly—Jeremy is hot. What is up with that? How and when did it happen?

"Kind of crazy, huh?"

This time I jump at the sound of the Girl in Black's voice.

I spin around and she's standing next to me again. Except she's changed outfits. For the first time on this whole journey or whatever it is, she's not dressed in black jeans and boots. No, instead she's in a ball gown. The thing is stunning—black, of course, and silky with sequins and feathers sewn into the bodice. She looks even more beautiful than before, not that I'm about to say so.

"Decided to dress up for the dance?" I ask, eyebrows raised.

She grins at me like she knows something I don't. "You could say that, I suppose."

"Right. That's why I just said it," I snap. And I turn back to future me and Jeremy. Something is about to happen. I can feel it in my bones.

"Turned out pretty cute, huh? Do you regret being so nasty to him before?" asks the Girl in Black.

"Hey, should I still call you the Girl in Black? Or are you now the Girl in the Black Prom Dress?" I wonder.

"You never answered my question," she replies.

"Oh, you're being serious about regrets?" I ask. "Okay, let me think about it for half a second. My answer is no. Not at all. I had a job to do and I did it well. Anyway, I couldn't have been so bad, so damaging. Look at how he's forgiven me. We are a great couple. We look amazing together."

I gesture toward the two teenagers, wondering why I feel the need to convince her when the proof is standing right there, walking and talking right in front of our eyes.

"I hope you've been practicing the dip for the victory dance," future me warns. "Because if you drop me I'm seriously going to kill you."

Jeremy laughs as if she is kidding, but I know she's not.

"We don't know for a fact that we are going to win," he says.

"Does that mean you haven't practiced, Jeremy? Big mistake. I don't know what you're thinking. Who else would win? No one is better than me. And I did choose you as my boyfriend, so you'll win by proxy. We look amazing. And this dress? It was designed in Paris. I should win for that alone."

Wait, have I been to Paris? Have I been to Paris to shop for a dress? My whole future keeps looking better and better.

Suddenly a phone rings. Future me slips it out from somewhere within the folds of her dress—a secret pocket. How cool! And even better, the phone actually matches the dress—all silver and iridescent.

"Yes, please deliver the ice sculpture at ten p.m., exactly," future me says before hanging up.

"Who was that?" Jeremy asks.

"The caterers for the after-party. We are doing an ice sculpture in the shape of the two of us. It's a surprise."

"Not anymore," says Jeremy.

Future me rolls her eyes. "I mean it's a surprise for

everyone else. You know what I mean. She hits him on the chest—lightly, playfully. He frowns. I recognize that frown. It travels up to his eyes, which look troubled. Pained, even. His whole expression tells me things aren't so perfect. Jeremy seems annoyed.

Oh well. I'm sure that happens a lot in relationships. After all, I'm only thirteen. I don't know what it's like to be in high school, or to have a high school boyfriend. I'm sure there are all kinds of nuances. Maybe tip-of-the-nose kissing is totally trending here in the future. It's probably a good way to keep germs from spreading.

I look around the gym. That's when I notice the posters onstage. It's the nominees for prom queen and king: four gorgeous girls and four hunky guys.

The gym is still empty, so I hop onstage and take a closer look.

The first nominee is me, of course. And I must be honest. I am completely, 100 percent blown away. My future self is stunning in person, but in pictures she is perfection. It's a casual shot. I'm in designer jeans, expensive-looking brown boots, and a red V-neck sweater. My hair is smooth and silky, like I've gotten a really great blowout. I look smart and sharp. I'm impressed with myself. I wonder where I'm going to college. Stanford or Princeton or Berkeley or Yale? I wonder what kind of car

I have—an SUV or something in the race car variety? Hopefully I'll get to find out.

I wander over to check out the other nominees. They surprise me. Harper is up there, for example. She looks good. Her hair is full-on black now, and super dramatic. Her smile is slightly uneven, higher on one side. And her eyelashes are long and thick. I wonder if they're fake. She's wearing a white minidress and strappy sandals. For a moment I'm annoyed that she made the cut. But then I realize that there have to be other nominees. They can't simply hand me the crown without holding elections, even though it's obvious I am the only one who deserves it. That must be why Maddie is pictured here, as well. At first glance I don't realize it's her, because her hair, once red and curly, is now brown and stick-straight. But I'd recognize her green eyes anywhere. She looks nice but a little too close to average. I'm sure she was very low-ranked. I hope she got a few votes, at least.

As soon as this thought pops into my brain I laugh it off. It's not true. I actually hope she got zero votes. Being selected as prom queen isn't good enough. I really need to win that crown in a landslide.

The next and final nominee for prom queen is shocking. It's Reese, the theater geek who made the murals back in the eighth grade. She really has changed. Her style is quirky and cute. Art-geek chic, I'd call it. She's wearing black, chunky glasses and she has a dirty-blond bob. She's in jeans and hiking boots and a navy-blue, over-sized sweater. Squinting at her photo more closely, I see that she isn't even wearing makeup. I can't believe that's the picture she submitted. I wonder if she was nominated as a joke. Probably. How sad.

The four prom king nominees are dressed basically the same, all of them wear jeans, and button-down shirts, and bright smiles. Jeremy and three other guys I don't recognize. The one named Nadir has dark skin and soulful brown eyes. Aidan is blond and preppy-looking. He's holding a football tucked under his arm. Theo is tall and thin with a bright smile and locs that almost reach his shoulders.

I wander back over to my future self, who is still in conversation with Jeremy.

"Hey, where is my corsage? You didn't forget it, did you? Because we can probably still get one last minute. If the flower shop is closed, one of my friends will give me theirs. Be honest. Okay?"

Jeremy looks uncomfortable suddenly. I smell trouble and future me does, too.

"Um, actually, Ellie. I need to talk to you about

something," Jeremy says, shifting nervously from one foot to the other.

He gives her a tortured sort of look, then glances down at his feet, like suddenly he's afraid to make eye contact. "Look, I hate to do this tonight, but, well . . . I think we need to break up."

She laughs. "Very funny."

"I'm not kidding," he says. And I can tell from his serious expression that he's not. "And when I say I think we should break up, well, what I actually mean is, we need to break up. We are breaking up. Technically, I suppose, we are broken up. Things are over. Done. I simply can't handle the pressure anymore."

"No. There's no way you can do this."

Both thirteen-year-old me and future me are speaking at the exact same time.

And suddenly the Girl in Black appears next to me again. I didn't even notice she'd left, but I'm grateful she's back.

I turn to her. "What is going on?" I ask. "This can't be happening. This isn't real. This is totally bogus. My boyfriend is not breaking up with me hours before my senior prom."

The Girl in Black snaps her fingers. Future me and future Jeremy freeze. Time has stopped.

Then she glares at me. "Let me ask you something," she says. "You've been so obsessed with yourself you haven't even stopped to wonder who I am?"

"What do you mean?" I ask. "I've wondered plenty. It's a fact and you know it's true because you've been reading my mind."

"Right," she says with a nod. "Good point. Let me clarify. You're supposed to be so smart, I'm surprised you haven't figured out my true identity. I mean, don't you recognize me, Ellie?"

"No," I say. "Why, are you famous or something?"

She laughs. "No, I'm not famous but I did play a major role in your childhood. And you do know me. At least you used to. Think about it."

I don't know what she's talking about. Not at first. It simply doesn't register. But the longer I look at her, the more I mull it over in my mind. I'm getting the strangest sensation.

Her dark hair, the freckles, and the mischievous blue eyes. The way she seems to know me so well. Is it because, could she be from my past?

No.

"There's no way." I shake my head. I back up. But I have to ask. "Are you Marley Winters?"

"Yup," she says. "It's me."

Once I say her name, I know it's true. In fact, it seems painfully obvious. The Girl in Black is Marley, my former best friend. Somehow Marley, who was the sweetest person in the whole world, has become a ruthless chick who has been leading me on this journey and making snide and sarcastic comments along the way.

In other words, the girl I ghosted way back when is now actually a ghost? Marley's ghost? And she's come back to haunt me?

She's haunting me.

It's so obvious, I can't believe I didn't catch on sooner.

When we were younger Marley's face was round and soft, but it's changed shape over the years. It's now more narrow. She's got the same eyes, though, and the same smattering of freckles. She's different in other ways, as well. She seems so cool, so confident. I am kind of tempted to give her a high five. Way to go, shedding your goody-two-shoes ways. If you had this attitude back when we were eleven, maybe things could've been different.

"Wow, Marley. You really grew up. This is amazing," I tell her. "Um, we should totally hang out now."

"Ellie, you are unbelievable. Sure, you finished at the top of your class, but you can still be so dense sometimes. So clueless."

"What are you talking about?" I ask.

"Well, you actually don't exist here in the future yet. But me? I'm going to the dance."

I look around, shaking my head. "I am so confused right now."

She nods. "Yeah, I'll bet. It's hard to explain, so I'm going to have to show you," she tells me.

I have no idea what she's talking about, but I guess I'll find out soon enough.

She snaps her fingers again. Everyone in the room unfreezes.

Then she walks up to future me and future Jeremy and says hello.

"What are you doing here, Marley?" future me asks.

I cringe at her bossy tone, but it's not like I can do anything about it.

"You're supposed to be picking up dessert from the caterer," future me continues. "There's no way you could be back already, and if you are, where's all the food? Those bonbons will melt in the sun, so I hope you didn't leave them in the car."

"Oh, Ellie, I called the caterer and asked them to deliver." Marley links her arm in Jeremy's. "I'm here because we need to tell you something."

"Why are you touching my boyfriend?" future me asks angrily.

"I'm not your boyfriend anymore, remember?" Jeremy replies sadly. "I'm sorry, El. I wanted to wait until prom was over. I know it's so important to you. You seem to have a lot wrapped up in this whole crazy high school popularity thing. But I couldn't take it for any longer. Marley and I . . . Well, we didn't mean for this to happen, but we fell in love."

Wait, what? This is crazy. This cannot be happening.

"No," says future me.

"It's true," says Jeremy. "She's amazing. Well, you know, you used to be best friends. And I never knew her when we were younger. But ever since she transferred here at the beginning of the year—"

"Whatever," future me snaps, holding up her hand to silence him. "I don't need all the gory details and I refuse to accept it. This cannot be happening!"

Except it is. And worse than that—future me and invisible me have merged. We are the same person, and I am crying—tears of rage. I'm not going to stand for it!

I hurry over to the double doors of the gym and try to throw them open. They are locked. I press the handle and push hard, throwing my weight into them, but they don't budge. I bang on the door in frustration and yell, but nothing happens. So I turn around.

And find myself in another change of scene. Now prom is in full swing. I am still future me: high school senior, seventeen years old, freshly dumped and solo at my prom.

A band is onstage playing a slow song I don't even recognize. It must be new! As annoyed as I am over Jeremy, not to mention flabbergasted by this whole Marley/ Girl in Black situation, I am also so curious about how everyone has grown up.

People look so different in high school. Over in the corner, I notice my best friends: Harper, Sofia, Maddie, and Lily. Finally some friendly faces! I go right over to them.

"Hey, gals. Looking good," I say.

"You too," Harper says. "What's up with your eye makeup, though? Have you been crying?"

"Of course not," I say, rolling my eyes. "Didn't you see the latest runway shows from Paris? The runny mascara look is totally in right now."

"I saw it," says Lily.

"Me too," Sofia agrees.

"The room looks amazing," Maddie tells me. "Great work."

"I know," I say.

"Where's Jeremy?" Maddie asks.

"Dancing with Marley, his new girlfriend," I say bluntly.

"Wait, what?" asks Lily, wide eyed. "When did that happen?"

"He broke up with me this afternoon," I admit. "It was the weirdest thing."

This is a major understatement, obviously.

"Are you okay?" Harper asks stupidly.

"No, of course I'm not okay. It's prom and my boyfriend has left me for Marley Winters. Can you believe that?" I snap.

Harper looks down at the ground.

"What?" I ask.

"Honestly?" she replies. "I can believe it. You've been so awful to Jeremy, and to everyone. Can you blame him? We are sick of it. We're graduating soon and everyone is so excited to be free of you. It's too much."

This is nuts. I look to my friends. Lily is sneaking M&M's from her purse, avoiding all eye contact.

Maddie is nodding and Sofia stares at me coldly.

I'm about to tell these girls off, when suddenly the music cuts out and the bandleader makes an announcement. "It's time to crown the king and queen," she calls. "Please give a hand to Principal Hatcher."

Everyone turns toward the stage, where the school

principal is standing. "Welcome to your prom. Everyone looks gorgeous and you are all winners."

I snort. "Yeah, right."

"Be quiet, Ellie," says Lily, elbowing me. "Don't ruin this."

"Really?" I ask. "You just elbowed me?"

"Both of you cut it out," Harper snaps.

I don't even know what to say. Since when do my friends talk back to me like this? I turn toward the stage and listen.

"Of course, we can only have one prom king," Principal Hatcher says. "And his name is, let's see . . ." She fumbles as she opens up the envelope, squints at the page through her reading glasses and reads, "It's Jeremy Hinkey. Congratulations, Jeremy."

Everybody around me claps. People seem genuinely happy. I totally don't get it. They all must have seen Jeremy dancing with Marley. So how come people aren't outraged over how he treated me? My friends hardly blinked when I told them the news. Where is the anger? What happened to loyalty? Things are seriously amiss. I start to boo, but my friends hush me. It is so rude! "Cut it out," I say.

"Shut up, Ellie. You're embarrassing us," Sofia whispers.

"I'm embarrassing you?" I ask, outraged.

"Yes!" Harper agrees.

The rest of my crew looks on with hostility. I shake my head and sigh. This is so not even worth getting upset about. Who cares about Jeremy? No one even remembers their prom king. It's only the queen who matters.

When I win, I'm going to refuse to dance with him. That'll show him. He doesn't deserve me. I wonder what'll happen. Sure, he'll be mortified. But what else? Maybe he'll have to surrender his crown and then I can choose a different winner.

I scan the crowd in search of some contenders. But my eyes are drawn to Jeremy up onstage, and beaming. It is seriously annoying. How can he be happy about this when we just broke up? "Thanks, everyone," he says, waving to the cheering crowd. He puts the crown on his head. "It fits!"

People laugh. They love him.

I roll my eyes.

Principal Hatcher steps up to the microphone once more. "And now for prom queen. It was a close race, and the winner is: Reese Jeffries."

I plaster a smile on my face and start to move forward, but then stop myself. Did I hear that wrong? Did she say . . . Why didn't she say Ellie Charles? This has got to be a mistake. And a big one. Reese can't win.

I'm supposed to be the prom queen. I need it. When Reese shows up onstage I can hardly believe my eyes. That theater geek chick, who doesn't even bother with makeup? She is the winner? Sure, she has an interesting look. Her haircut is asymmetrical and her dress is made up of bold blocks of color. It's retro and outrageous in a good way. Also, she looks so . . . happy and confident and herself.

But this can't be how my story ends. I worked so hard to be the best. I deserve to be prom queen. Don't I?

It is so ironic and makes no sense at all: In trying so hard to win at life, to be the best, I've alienated everyone who matters. I am left with no one.

I have no friends.

I have no boyfriend.

From the way people avert their eyes when I try to make eye contact, it seems as if I am despised by everyone.

This is garbage! It can't be the real future. This cannot be the end of my story.

chapter thirteen

I bolt out of the gym and end up back in the bread. The tunnel is supposed to lead me somewhere, I'm sure, but there's nowhere I want to go right now. I'm too confused to move, so I lay down on my back and close my eyes and try to figure it all out. There's probably a reason I keep coming back here, to this bread tunnel. But what could it be?

I think about my life: past, present, future. Everything laid out in front of me. What Marley's ghost showed me and what she left out.

I think about the bread, when my mom and I used to make it. It's one of my happiest early memories. Baking bread with my mom, and sometimes with Marley, too. It always made me feel safe and warm and loved. It was a big part of my life. At one point. A long time ago. Why did I ever stop? Those nights were magical.

The three of us would listen to old music from when my mom was a teenager; all this classic eighties stuff that's fun to dance to: Prince, Cyndi Lauper, the Bangles, Tom Petty and the Heartbreakers. We had so much fun dancing around the kitchen, using wooden spoons as microphones. We didn't care about looking goofy, being embarrassing. That was kind of the point.

Every bread-baking session was a little different, but we always used the same starter. The one my mom made when I was a baby. We'd take a hunk off to make a new loaf. But the old starter stayed alive, kept growing. So in a sense, we were always starting from the same place.

What grew from there was up to us.

I think that I am kind of like that starter. I used to be sweet, and then life happened. As I grew up bad things happened to me. My dad left. Some girls were mean and felt sorry for me. I didn't get a bike on Christmas. (Sure, it arrived two weeks later, but at the time it wasn't good enough.) I was jealous of my sweet and smart and kind best friend, the girl with the smart and kind parents. I only focused on what I didn't have. I let those feelings of hurt and sadness fester into something ugly. And that ugliness grew and grew and it reproduced itself, and became something bigger and more fierce. A gigantic sourdough bread ball of horribleness.

I decided that being shy and sweet made me weak and I wanted to be strong. But when it came to standing up for my very best friend, the one who loved me for who I was, I did nothing. Which makes me the biggest coward imaginable.

Is that my only story, though? Is it who I am? Was this my only choice, or could I have grown up differently? I wonder if maybe I can do better. If I can be better.

And suddenly, after I have these thoughts, I open my eyes to find that the tunnel has disappeared. I am back in the kitchen—the original version with the yellow plaid wallpaper. The ingredients for bread are on the counter: flour, water, and a new mason jar. I look for the starter in the fridge but it's not there. The shelf is empty. The whole fridge is empty. I guess I'm starting from scratch.

As I take the ingredients, I realize it is all up to me. I need to bake this bread, to make this life by myself. As I mix, my fingers get wet and sticky and it feels good. And suddenly something occurs to me—the words seem to enter my head spontaneously: Be nice. Be a different person. Be better, nicer. I can't rewrite the past. I can change the future, though. Otherwise, well, what? I don't know. I'll be forced to relive my worst moments? Is that what I want to focus on? Is that what I want my story to be? Why do I even need to ask the question? I mean, duh! The answer is so obvious. Of course I don't.

This whole rant sounds corny. A week ago, I would've scoffed at such thoughts, but a week ago I didn't see what I've now seen.

The past is done. It was awful. I was awful. Yes, I'm ashamed. Of course I am. I'm not a monster.

But that's just it. I have been behaving like a monster. Is that what I'm supposed to regret? Is that the whole point of this?

I look up at the sky. I don't know if the Girl in Black, if Marley's ghost, or whatever she is can hear me, but I need to speak.

"I have been hideous and there are no excuses. I totally get that. I'm going to change, if I have a chance. Please give me a chance. I thought I was being brave but I was the biggest coward of all. I should've stood up for you. And failing that, I should've apologized. You were my true friend and I turned my back on you. It was wrong and it's no way to live. I don't blame you for haunting me. I ghosted you and that was terrible. I want to go back, to do things differently. I need to change my whole entire life."

Is this true? I think this is true.

I am crying now.

Tears stream down my face. I finish mixing the bread and I put the mound on a baking sheet and open up the oven.

Next thing I know, I'm back in the school gym, flat on my back.

chapter fourteen

When I open my eyes, I see concerned faces looking down at me. Harper and Sofia, Jack and Charlie.

I blink a few times and rub my eyes and realize I am back, finally.

I am thirteen years old, and we are hours away from the Winter Holiday Semiformal.

I try to stand up but I can't. Not by myself. Jack gives me a hand. I grab on to it and he pulls me up. I feel dizzy and my head is killing me. I have never been in this much pain.

Chloe and Jenna both reach out to steady me because I'm swaying, like I'm in danger of falling.

"Oh, thank you so much," I tell them, sincerely grateful.

They seem taken aback.

"What?" I ask.

"You're not mad?" asks Chloe, wide-eyed.

Jenna bites her bottom lip nervously. They expect me to scream and shout, I can tell. They are used to this atrocious behavior.

I smile at them. "No, I'm grateful to all of you. And I owe everyone a huge apology. I am so thankful to everyone who has worked so hard on this committee. The gym looks amazing. I don't know where I would be without you."

Jack looks at the committee. The theater geeks. Wait—I can't call them that anymore. I mean the theater *kids* look especially wary, and I don't blame them. I walk over to Reese.

She takes a step back, as if she's afraid of me. I guess she is afraid of me. And she has good reason to be.

"It's okay," I say, holding up my hands as if to surrender. "I promise I'm not going to hurt you. And I'm not going to destroy anything. Really. I just need to tell you something. That scene you created? It's gorgeous. I feel like I could step into it, truly. Looking at the mural, I can almost smell the fresh snow. Can you imagine zipping down a hill in one of those sleds? How exhilarating that would be? It's so lifelike. And what I said before? About the snowmen being too chubby? That was kind of crazy. And even the winter birds—they were stunning, better than anything I could've created. I wouldn't have even thought of it. I realize that now. I mean, I realized it at the time, too, but, well, sometimes I say things to get a reaction. It's like I'm a parody of a mean girl. It became kind of a game. How cruel could I be? What could I get away with? And the answer? Way too much. There was no limit, actually."

"What's she talking about?" Reese asks Jack, who shrugs.

I continue. "What I mean to say is, well, I'm sorry I ripped up your poster. That was horrible of me. I truly regret my actions. I know you think I'm this certain type of girl. The way I act? It's been awful. And I've been watching myself in the past. I mean, um, thinking about my behavior . . ."

Reese looks like she doesn't believe me.

I can't blame her. I reach out to touch her arm and she flinches.

Does she actually think I would physically hurt her?

She really does.

I have a lot of work to do.

I look at the other kids. "You guys, I know I've been awful. And not just today. I mean for years."

Some of them stare at me. Some look at each other nervously. No one says a word. What is there to say? Are they too shocked? Do they think it's a trick?

No one denies what I'm saying. No one goes, "That's okay, Ellie. We know you didn't mean it."

Instead they stare at me, dumbfounded.

And there are sirens in the distance. I turn my head toward the noise.

"Oh, the ambulance must be close," says Jack.

"The ambulance," I repeat.

"We called it after you fell," Jack explains. "You were out for so long, like, more than five minutes."

"I was terrified," says Harper.

"Me too. I lost my appetite over it," Lily tells me.

"Should we call it off?" Jack asks.

"Yes," I say. "Definitely. I don't need it."

He whips his phone out of his pocket and starts to dial, but Reese puts her hand on his arm, stopping him.

"Wait," she says, her voice a mere whisper. "I think we should wait for medical professionals."

"But I'm fine," I say, grinning wildly.

She looks at me worriedly. "Are you sure, Ellie?"

"Of course," I say. And it's true. I'm feeling great. "I couldn't be better. Why do you ask?"

"Um, it's just that, well, you're acting a little weird."

She seems afraid to say this, like I'm going to jump down her throat. And I can't blame her hesitation. The old me would've been on the attack for her merely second-guessing me. But now, well, obviously I'm a changed girl. I've been scared straight. "You guys. I'm completely fine, but thank you for the concern."

"I think something happened to her when she fell. She should be examined," Chloe says.

The sirens are getting louder. The ambulance must be right around the corner. Before it gets any closer, I run out of the gym.

chapter fifteen

I don't stop running until I'm two blocks from school. Then, out of breath and with aching legs, I sit down on the sidewalk behind a moving van that blocks me from view. Then I pull out my phone and call my father. He's expecting me in Hawaii tomorrow, but there's no way I am stepping onto that plane. It's not simply because I know what a disastrous time I'd have. There's a lot more to it than that. I can't abandon my mom on Christmas. I won't. It's wrong. And she deserves so much more. I've been rotten to her and that's got to stop.

And as for my dad, well, it's more complicated. I need to try to change how things are going, try to make him understand who I am and how hurt I've been by how he treats me.

I dial my dad's cell and luckily, he actually takes my call. A good sign!

"Ellie, everything okay?" he asks me. "I thought you were busy getting ready for that dance."

"Yes, I am," I tell him. "Thanks for remembering." This is no time for small talk. I've got a lot of work to do, so I cut to the chase. "Dad, I really appreciate your invitation, but I'm not going to meet you in Hawaii tomorrow. I can't leave Mom on Christmas. It wouldn't be fair. She's stuck by me all these years."

"But we have to talk about something important," my dad says.

"I know," I say. "Believe me, I know. And you are absolutely right. We do need to talk about a lot of things. Except can we do it another time? Like next week? I'm totally free. I can meet you in Hawaii. Actually, no, that's not right. Why don't you come here? You haven't been to Lincoln Heights in ages."

"Ellie, you know how busy I am . . ."

"And you know that I am your only daughter," I reply. "And you should be around more. It's not fair to me. I know you have big news. Life-altering stuff. And I need to tell you, Dad. You're making a gigantic mistake. Nikka is not who you think she is."

"What are you talking about? This is nonsense. How do you even know about Nikka?"

"Oh, um, I guess you must've mentioned her before at some point."

"No, I haven't. And you've never even met her. I only met her a month ago."

"Wow, that's even crazier, Dad."

"Not for you to say, Ellie. And it's not the point. Please tell me how you know about this. It's all very confusing."

"I'll explain later," I tell him. "Maybe."

"Well, what am I supposed to do with your suite?" he asks. "It's got ocean views, Ellie. Do you realize what a big deal that is?"

This fancy vacation seemed so great the first time around. Now the whole thing sounds pathetic, desperate. How can an expensive hotel suite make up for years of neglect? It cannot. I'm not going to pretend like it will. I won't fall for it. I cannot be bribed like this.

"I'm sure it's beautiful, but I am also sure that you're going to be in Denmark for some emergency, anyway, so what's the point?"

My dad doesn't say anything for a moment. Then he sighs. "Ellie honey, I don't understand what you're talking about. Where are you getting this information? How do you even know that I'm working on a project in Denmark? And Nikka? Who have you been speaking with? What is going on here?"

"There's no time to explain now, so let me just say this: You only live a few hours away, and I never get to see you. I don't need to fly across an ocean to not see you. And even if you were going to be there? It's not good enough. I try so hard to be perfect, to be everything, and none of it matters. I can't change who you are or how you treat me. And I shouldn't have to work so hard to try to change myself into the girl you want me to be."

"Okay, I see," he replies carefully.

It is so frustrating, this whole thing!

"But you don't, Dad. That's the problem. You never see. Not me. Not Mom. Not our reality—how things really are. And I wish you would. But I'm done trying. I don't want to be like you. It's not worth it."

"Oh, Ellie."

His voice makes me question everything, but I need to stand my ground. These are things that need to be said. And that's all that I can do for now. "Merry Christmas, Dad. Let's talk soon."

As soon as I hang up, I put my phone away.

I feel better, but my work isn't done. I sprint to Jeremy

Hinkey's house and bang on his front door. Lucky for me, it's only a few blocks away.

Jeremy opens it up but as soon as he realizes it's me, he tries to slam the door in my face.

Interesting and not totally shocking, I suppose. Still, I am not going to give up that easily. I manage to kick my foot inside the entryway, jamming the door so it doesn't close entirely.

Ouch, that hurts.

I gulp and try not to focus on the pain. There are more important things!

"Wait! We need to talk. Don't be scared," I say, because I see a lot of fear in his eyes. That kind of thing used to bring me pride. Now I only feel embarrassment and shame.

"I promise I'm not going to hurt you, Jeremy. I'm here to apologize."

He scoffs. "Yeah right. Ellie Charles apologize? Do you think I'm stupid? Because I'm not stupid."

"I don't think you're stupid. In fact, I know you are not stupid. And I know you didn't fart. Remember, from the meeting way back when?"

"You mean earlier today?" asks Jeremy.

"Right," I say. "Earlier today. I have grown a lot in that time. In fact, I'm a whole new girl. It's complicated so don't ask. Anyway, I'm sorry I embarrassed you. It was mean and completely gratuitous. I've had a lot of time to think about my behavior and I want to apologize. No, I need to apologize. Not only for the fart lie. But for being so hard on you about the snacks. I don't know why I was so difficult, so cruel. No, that's not true. I did it to make you look bad, so I would seem better, more in control, the one with all the answers. And that was wrong, and I'm sorry. Truly."

I look him in the eye, hoping he will accept my bizarre and hard-to-believe transformation.

"What's the catch?" he asks tiredly. "Why don't you tell me now and save me the trouble?"

"There's no catch, I swear. And I don't blame you for not trusting me. I have been horrible to you. To everyone, actually. You don't need to believe me, but I need to say it. I'm so sorry, Jeremy. I hope that someday you'll forgive me. And I hope to see you at the dance."

I turn around and leave before he can argue. Before he can ask me any more questions.

It feels good, coming clean like this. I feel lighter, freer, somehow. But then I realize I'm not done. Not by a long stretch.

There's something else I need to do. Something more important.

It's not Marley's fault that she has a perfect life. Two awesome dads while I have none. It's not her fault that my dad left my mom. Left me.

Marley has always been there for me. She's always been a good and true friend. And the way I treated her? She didn't deserve it. She didn't deserve any of it. And I've been a big coward, not saying anything. Letting things go on like this for so many years. Everything was my fault—I see that now. I thought I was being brave by acting tough, by focusing on being the best and the strongest. When actually I've been a huge coward, and enough is enough.

I head to Marley's place next, and I knock on her door. Marley answers but—what a coincidence—she has no interest in speaking to me, either. For the second time today, someone slams the door on me.

And for the second time today, I cannot blame them in the least.

But I'm not going to give up so easily.

When a door slams in your face, find a window. That phrase pops into my head. And I take it as a sign. I try all the windows in the house, but they are locked. I pick up a rock, pull back my arm and aim for the glass, but then I have second thoughts . . .

Sure, I have something I need to say, but maybe a forceful approach isn't necessary.

That's why I scale her backyard fence and then crawl inside her house through the doggie door.

"I'm going to call the police," Marley threatens as soon as she realizes what I've done.

"No wait!" I say, holding up my hands. "Please hear me out. Give me five minutes. I'm begging you. I'm haunted by this. Please, Marley. For old times' sake?"

"Do you promise you're going to leave after five minutes?" she asks.

"Of course," I say. I hold up my right pinky. "Pinky swear."

"Ellie, we are not eight years old anymore. Pinky swears are for babies."

"I know that," I say. "But it's kind of perfect because I've been acting so childish and immature. I know I was horrible to you, and then, on top of it, I ghosted you. It was pathetic. But I was so mad I wasn't seeing things clearly. I didn't blame myself and I should have. I was the worst."

I think I've gotten to her, a little. She doesn't respond with words, but something in her disdainful expression softens ever so slightly.

So I open up further, trying to explain. "I was so jealous of you. You had everything—you're smarter than me and better and stronger. You know who you are and you don't care what people think. Meanwhile, you are so good. You were always there for me. Always stood by me. The most loyal friend. Even when I was horrible to you. You forgave me and were willing to give me another chance. It was too much. And I couldn't stand it. So I lashed out. It was pathetic. You were a good friend and I ruined everything out of spite. I'm so sorry."

It's too little too late. I know this, and I can tell that Marley is still angry.

"You can't change the past," she tells me pointedly. "You totally betrayed me by sending that stupid video of me. And you knew it was a joke but when all those kids made fun of me, you just stood there. You said nothing. You shut me out. And then, when I was willing to forgive you, you didn't even bother to apologize. You ignored me."

"I was weak. I am weak. I'm sorry." This is not only the truth, it's also the only thing I can think to say.

"You have no idea how mortified I was. It has ruined my whole entire life!"

"Is that true?" I ask. "Because you look pretty happy now."

"Well, yes, because you are out of my life," Marley says. "And it took me a long time to get to this point. What you did? It was beyond humiliating. It's the worst thing that's ever happened to me. And I'm not even talking about the stupid video. I'm over that. The thing that really stung? It was your betrayal. Because you are the one I cared about and you abandoned me. We were best friends and you turned on me. You didn't stick up for me. And then you ghosted me."

"You're right," I say. "I have no idea what you went through, so maybe it's time I find out."

Marley seems confused and I don't blame her. This whole thing is kind of crazy, so unlike me. But sometimes crazy is necessary. I have spent too much time plotting and planning. All this conniving to get me to the top? It worked, but it's a sad and lonely place to be. What is the end? Where do I go from here? This is not simply because my life turns out rotten. Not simply because Marley stole my boyfriend, and Reese stole my crown, and everyone secretly hates me except it's not even a secret anymore.

These thoughts race through my head, all of them so jumbled. I am not sure how to explain but I need to try, so I take a deep breath and go for it.

"Okay," I tell her. "It's like this. You can look at the world and think, 'How can I make this a better place?' Or you can go out into the world and do what's best for yourself, regardless of who you hurt, who you trample on, or other people's feelings. I want to be the first kind of person. Because the second kind, well, I've tried it out and I can tell you from experience—while it appears super fun, it's been miserable. I'm talking 'slowly chipping away at your soul' misery. The kind you don't even realize is happening until it's too late. There are other, better ways of being in the world. I want to be kind and generous and good. I want to make stuff, like sourdough bread and art and happiness. I've wasted so much time focused on all the wrong things. Manufacturing misery. In myself and others. And it's been awful. It's simply an awful way to be. I see that now. It's lonely at the top. I always thought that was some dumb phrase made up by losers so they wouldn't feel bad about themselves for not being the best. But I can tell you, I have worked hard to claw my way to the top and it's true. It's lonely and no good."

She stares at me for a long time without saying anything.

"What?" I ask her.

Twisting her mouth up, she tilts her head to one side and inhales deeply before speaking. "It's weird, because you sound so sincere."

"I am being sincere," I promise. "Oh, and there's one more thing. I also believe in justice. And sometimes that means revenge."

I hand my phone to Marley. "Go ahead and turn it on," I tell her.

She rolls her eyes at me. "You're still trying to micromanage everything, Ellie. And I am not playing this game. I have zero interest. You are totally right. There are people you meet in life who make you feel better, who do good things, who make the world a better place. But I know you and I think you make the world a *worse* place. And I'm sick of it. I don't want to care anymore. I don't want to have anything to do with you." She tries to hand me back my phone, but I refuse to take it.

Instead I start to tap dance. Except I don't really know how to tap dance. And I haven't tried to do any type of dance in the longest time. It's been years, actually. So I look kind of foolish.

Marley is unimpressed, but at least I have her attention now.

"I am sorry, Marley. You are right. But please go ahead and record this. I have something I need to get off my chest."

She rolls her eyes. "This is ridiculous."

"I know, but please humor me."

"Do you promise to go away after this?" she asks.

"Yes," I say. "As long as you press record."

"Don't tell me what to do," she replies. But she goes

ahead and presses the right button and holds up the phone so it's trained on my face.

"This is a video of the real me. I'm sad most of the time. My parents went through an ugly divorce. My dad is a jerk, but I took his side because he bought me more stuff. I learned how to be awful to my friends and I have betrayed everyone. I talk about people behind their backs. The reason I make fun of other kids dancing is because I'm jealous of their confidence, of the way they can let loose and be totally free, themselves, goofy, whatever. And I'm going to prove it."

With that, I start break dancing. Attempting to break dance, I mean. It's a joke. I look ridiculous.

Marley, who hasn't cracked a smile since she laid eyes on me, is actually grinning.

I stop for a moment and continue. "Also? I have a massive crush on Jeremy Hinkey, who will probably grow up and break my heart. Not now. In the future. Trust me! I'm going to be bonkers for the guy."

"Is that everything?" asks Marley.

"Isn't that enough?" I ask.

"Why don't you do another dance?" asks Marley.

"Okay." I pretend my body is a wet noodle and shake.

"I said do a dance, not have a seizure," says Marley.

"Honestly, it's all the same for me," I huff, out of breath and a little sweaty.

She lowers my phone.

"Okay. Go ahead and send that to everyone in my contacts. Or better yet, put it on Instagram. I have more than a thousand followers. And I deserve to be embarrassed in front of everyone."

Marley looks at my phone. "You'd do that for me, just so I'll forgive you?"

"Of course," I say, gulping. "Go ahead. You should have your revenge. You've totally earned it. I was horrible to you."

Marley shakes her head and says, "No, Ellie. That's okay. It's enough that you'd be willing to sacrifice your entire reputation. I know how much it means to you. Plus, I'm not going to stoop to your level."

"Really?" I ask. "You are incredible. I don't know what to say."

"Why don't you say this: Two wrongs don't make a right. Because it's not about revenge. It's about owning up to your mistakes and apologizing and living with them," Marley tells me. "It's about striving to be a better person. Which you are going to start doing. Immediately."

She hands me my phone and I look at it, half expecting her to have posted the video even though she refused. But when I look at it more carefully, I see that she hasn't even recorded anything.

I glance up at her.

She is quiet, thinking. It makes me nervous. And then I have another idea.

"Hey, want to come to the dance with me? Our future boyfriend is going to be there. I mean, if he forgives me for embarrassing him a little while ago."

"What are you talking about?" Marley asks.

"You'll see," I reply. "Just come."

Marley shakes her head. "I don't want to go to a dance tonight, to see all those people. I've moved on."

"Well, what about me?" I ask. "I mean, obviously you've moved on from me, too. But do you think you can ever forgive me? Do you think we can be friends again?"

She stares at me for a long time and then grins. "I'll think about it."

"Okay, well, I'll call you tomorrow. See how you're feeling, and hope you can forgive me. Thank you for listening to me. You're a bigger person than me. And I've missed you."

"I've missed you, too," she says. She reaches out and gives me a hug.

And that seems like a good start.

chapter sixteen

I have been through these gym doors so many times lately, with no idea what I'd find on the other side. But tonight feels different.

I'm a little late and the music is already playing. I glance around the room and notice the flaws: One of the corners of the murals is coming down and the string lights by the fire exit are sagging. Before the fall, I'd find someone from my committee and scream at them, maybe kick them out of the dance. But now I know it's not worth it.

And speaking of kicking people out of the dance, I spot Jeremy Hinkey in the corner by the sliced veggies. He's wearing a striped shirt and a bow tie, looking at me nervously. Like he expects me to kick him out of the dance, or perhaps to simply kick him. I go over and say hello.

"You look great," I tell him.

"Um, so I can stay?" he asks.

"Of course," I reply. "And sorry again."

"You're weird," he says.

"I know," I say. "Sometimes weird is good, though. Right?"

"Whatever you say," he replies, and walks away.

Just then I feel someone yank me by the elbow. It's Harper. "What is he doing here?" she asks me. "Do you want me to tell him to leave?"

"No, it's okay," I say.

"Okay, fine. Well, I'm glad you are finally here. You're not going to believe what happened to Lily. She tried to flatten her hair with a flat iron and she singed some of it off."

"That's awful," I say.

"No, it's hilarious," she says.

I shake my head. "No, I feel terrible. Poor girl."

"What is up with you?" Harper asks me.

I don't even want to get into it and one of my favorite songs is playing. Usually I'd hang back with my friends and we'd make fun of other people dancing, but tonight I have a new idea.

I dance. All by myself.

Sure, Marley refused to tape my performance, but I still feel the need to do something bold. So I pretend like I am dancing for the camera, acting wacky and crazy and embarrassing.

People gather around me to watch, but no one gets too close. The crowd is unsure of what to make of me. So I decide to give them a show—I don't even need to try to dance badly, to embarrass myself. It happens naturally.

And now that I've let my guard down, people are whispering and pointing, and eventually laughing. And it's weird because people haven't laughed at me in years. But it's also okay, because I deserve it. Plus, it's not so bad. There are worse things. Like living your life to be cruel and thoughtless. Hurting other people. Becoming rotten inside.

I'm starting all over. With a new starter.

Two songs later, I'm sweating up a storm, so I take a break to have some water. There are lemon slices floating around on top. I would've thrown in some cucumber, too. Maybe even some mint but, no biggie, this will do just fine. I take a sip. It's refreshing.

Glancing around the gym, I feel truly happy—at peace. The room looks spectacular, not because I was in charge of the committee, but because everyone else worked together to create something magical.

It reminds me of happier, simpler times. And for the first time in ages, I'm excited for Christmas, for spending time with my mom, to whom I owe not only a huge apology, but also a major attitude adjustment.

And thinking about all this makes me wonder, was this all a dream? Did I simply fall too hard and hit my head and imagine everything?

I stare up at the disco ball. It's a little off-center but still looks great. And then I see her—Marley Winters, the Girl in Black. She's in those little mirrored squares—hundreds of her. And then the images go away and the disco ball turns into a crystal ball. Marley's face fills up the entire globe. She's looking down and smiling.

I wink at her and she winks back. And then I set down my drink and head back to the dance floor. I know I've still got a lot of work to do.

For now, though, I'm going to keep on dancing.

Acknowledgments

Thanks so much to everyone who helped make this novel possible, and special thanks to my beta readers, who made it a lot better: Dinah Yorkin, Georgia Gray, Marly Moore, Molly Shayne, Leo Margolis, and Lucy Margolis. Thanks, also, to Jim Margolis, Bhargavi Sylbert, Katherine Cortas, Laura Langlie, and the fabulous people at FSG, including Janine O'Malley, Melissa Warten, Heather Job, and Mary Van Akin.